HE TURNED.

Not even the man's jacket she was wearing could thin down the look of her lush body.

"John, I'll ride with you."

"What'll you do when we get there?"

"I'm like a cat," said Molly. "I always land on my feet. Maybe start a high-class whorehouse. Save up enough to retire on."

Slocum admired her. She had spoken without any self-pity.

"O.K.," he said finally. "We got some hard riding. They must know by now we've gone."

OTHER BOOKS BY JAKE LOGAN

RIDE, SLOCUM, RIDE
HANGING JUSTICE
SLOCUM AND THE WIDOW
    KATE
ACROSS THE RIO GRANDE
THE COMANCHE'S WOMAN
SLOCUM'S GOLD
BLOODY TRAIL TO TEXAS
NORTH TO DAKOTA
SLOCUM'S WOMAN
WHITE HELL
RIDE FOR REVENGE
OUTLAW BLOOD
MONTANA SHOWDOWN
SEE TEXAS AND DIE
IRON MUSTANG
SHOTGUNS FROM HELL
SLOCUM'S BLOOD
SLOCUM'S FIRE
SLOCUM'S REVENGE
SLOCUM'S HELL
SLOCUM'S GRAVE
DEAD MAN'S HAND
FIGHTING VENGEANCE
SLOCUM'S SLAUGHTER
ROUGHRIDER
SLOCUM'S RAGE
HELLFIRE
SLOCUM'S CODE
SLOCUM'S FLAG
SLOCUM'S RAID
SLOCUM'S RUN
BLAZING GUNS
SLOCUM'S GAMBLE
SLOCUM'S DEBT
SLOCUM AND THE MAD MAJOR
THE NECKTIE PARTY
THE CANYON BUNCH
SWAMP FOXES
LAW COMES TO COLD RAIN
SLOCUM'S DRIVE
JACKSON HOLE TROUBLE

SILVER CITY SHOOTOUT
SLOCUM AND THE LAW
APACHE SUNRISE
SLOCUM'S JUSTICE
NEBRASKA BURNOUT
SLOCUM AND THE CATTLE
    QUEEN
SLOCUM'S WOMEN
SLOCUM'S COMMAND
SLOCUM GETS EVEN
SLOCUM AND THE LOST DUTCHMAN
    MINE
HIGH COUNTRY HOLDUP
GUNS OF SOUTH PASS
SLOCUM AND THE HATCHET
    MEN
BANDIT GOLD
SOUTH OF THE BORDER
DALLAS MADAM
TEXAS SHOWDOWN
SLOCUM IN DEADWOOD
SLOCUM'S WINNING HAND
SLOCUM AND THE GUN RUNNERS
SLOCUM'S PRIDE
SLOCUM'S CRIME
THE NEVADA SWINDLE
SLOCUM'S GOOD DEED
SLOCUM'S STAMPEDE
GUNPLAY AT HOBBS' HOLE
THE JOURNEY OF DEATH
SLOCUM AND THE AVENGING GUN
SLOCUM RIDES ALONE
THE SUNSHINE BASIN WAR
VIGILANTE JUSTICE
JAILBREAK MOON
SIX-GUN BRIDE
MESCALERO DAWN
DENVER GOLD
SLOCUM AND THE BOZEMAN TRAIL
SLOCUM AND THE HORSE THIEVES
SLOCUM AND THE NOOSE OF HELL
CHEYENNE BLOODBATH

JAKE LOGAN

THE BLACKMAIL EXPRESS

BERKLEY BOOKS, NEW YORK

THE BLACKMAIL EXPRESS

A Berkley Book/published by arrangement with
the author

PRINTING HISTORY
Berkley edition / July 1986

ISBN: 0-425-09088-4

A BERKLEY BOOK® TM 757,375
Berkley Books are published by The Berkley Publishing Group,
200 Madison Avenue, New York, NY 10016.
The name "BERKLEY"and the stylized "B" with design are trademarks
belonging to Berkley Publishing Corporation.

PRINTED IN THE UNITED STATES OF AMERICA

1

Slocum very gently set down the bottle of nitroglycerin on top of J. J. Taylor. J. J. Taylor was a square safe that weighed nine hundred and fifty pounds. The nitro filled three-quarters of a blue glass medicine bottle. The rest of the bottle was filled with water; this prevented the nitro—a notoriously unstable animal—from sloshing around, with a resulting violent explosion which could blow apart a man who might be carrying it in his pocket.

Inside the safe was Joe Gill's weekly receipts from the saloon and gambling house that occupied the premises downstairs. Beside the safe was Gill's oak desk and a swivel chair. Across the room, resting on a fine rug, was Gill's office bed. He used it for impromptu affairs with the girls who worked for him in his dance hall. They were usually afraid to say no.

The saloon was closed for the night. It was almost

four-thirty in the morning and it was raining like hell. Lightning flared and thunder crashed and boomed over the Sangre de Cristo range, the mountain chain that framed Santa Fe to the east. When the lightning flared the thunder reverberated through the town. Slocum had waited almost three weeks for such a noisy night.

Slocum despised Joe Gill. Gill was a hard, unscrupulous, handsome man of thirty-seven. He wore a luxurious black mustache, and his broad, fleshy face was beginning to run to fat. He had well-manicured hands and he dressed with expensive taste. Gill ran a crooked gambling house. He had started life as a pimp in New Orleans at the age of twenty-four. He seduced and then supplied the girls to the Yankee Army of Occupation when the War ended. Later, he made his way westward with a traveling whorehouse. He followed the Union Pacific as it built westward from Omaha. He would set up his wagon at the head of the tracks; next to it would be a plank stretched across two kegs of cheap whiskey. By the time the tracks reached Promontory Point in 1869 he had put aside over seventy thousand dollars. Much of it came from the crooked decks; more came from rolling drunken railroaders.

With the proceeds he bought a big house on Galisteo Street in Santa Fe, two short blocks from the Plaza. He turned it into a gambling house and dance hall which attracted a great many people. The games were crooked, but Joe Gill didn't care as long as he got his fifteen percent cut from the professional card players who dealt faro and poker.

Then one Friday night John Slocum entered Joe Gill's saloon. Gill sat at a card table smoking an expensive cigar. Slocum had four hundred and twenty-three dollars, the proceeds of a post office robbery in Ely, Nevada. Slocum asked if he could sit in.

"Suit yourself," Gill grunted.

Within five minutes Slocum saw that Gill was an expert card mechanic. He did false shuffles. He dealt himself key cards from the bottom of the deck. Not only that, Slocum had noticed that as soon as he had dealt the hands he looked narrowly at the backs of the cards in the other players' hands. He did not look at his own cards right away. Slocum knew that Gill was using a marked deck.

For a brief moment Slocum had considered pointing out this interesting fact to Gill. Then a gunman, clearly in Gill's employ, went to each of the four busy cash registers set behind the very busy bar and collected the proceeds. He placed them in a small but strong canvas sack. He only picked up the bills and gold coins. Silver was left behind. Then the collector walked upstairs.

Slocum wondered if he should refer to Gill's cheating. Gill would deny it, and there would probably be gunplay. With Gill's gunmen hanging around—and they looked competent—the issue might be in doubt. There had to be plenty of them lounging around, simply because of the fifteen gaming tables and the huge piles of gold coins and bills of large denominations.

Slocum decided that it would be better taste for him to extract the money Gill had swindled from him, as well as everyone else's, from the safe upstairs. There had to be a safe upstairs. Gill was not the type to sit over all that cash with a shotgun all night waiting for his bank to open.

Slocum decided to hang around, play some more poker, find out exactly where the safe was and what kind it was, and then blow it.

For this he needed two things: nitroglycerin and a night full of thunder. The nitro for a jam shot, in which the door would be blown neatly off its hinges. Thunder would camouflage the dull boom of the explosion.

Slocum stayed in the game. He amused himself by trying to find out how the cards were marked. He finally discovered that the back of each card had ten flowers. Each flower had six petals. It had been easy for Gill to shade each of the petals in such a way that the fifty-two cards in the deck could all be identified. Of course, there were complications to the design, arabesques and curlicues preventing any casual observer from realizing that each card had been tampered with.

Once Slocum had solved the technique, he stayed in. He could have started to win, but he did not want Gill to become suspicious. So he lost a little and won a little. He wanted to hang around till he had found out about the safe upstairs.

He had planned to ride out of Santa Fe in the morning. But now he decided to take a room and wait for a night full of thunder.

Slocum had been planning to spend the night in a cheap hotel, then ride up to Colorado along the Gunnison River. There were some rich ranches there and he knew where he could pick up a couple of people and then run the cattle up into Wyoming, where they were busily stocking new ranches and wouldn't ask embarrassing questions.

Instead he took a furnished room with a landlady who had the improbable name of Desdemona Jenkins. Her house was on Grant Avenue, a few short blocks away from Joe Gill's place on the far side of the Plaza. She was a horse-faced, sour woman of sixty who had been in the theater as a Shakespearean actress, and had taken her first name from the heroine she most admired.

Slocum told her that he had quit his job at ranch on the Rio Chama and wanted to take it easy for a couple of weeks. He gave her three weeks' rent in advance with the explanation that he would probably stay for that long. Her face fell into amiable lines, and she invited him to take a cup of tea with her any time he passed by. He told her the idea of a soft mattress and four walls for a while had a mighty strong appeal.

Slocum found a cheap livery stable in an alley that connected Grant and Lincoln Avenues. The charge to board his roan gelding was a dollar a day. There was no charge for storing his saddle and horse gear in the tack room.

Slocum began to spend most of his time at Joe Gill's. He ate at a Mexican restaurant on the east side of the Plaza. He took his dirty laundry to Yum Kee, on Lincoln Avenue.

Every evening for the next two weeks Slocum gambled at Joe Gill's place. Gill began to like this tall green-eyed man who never complained when he lost and never became drunk or unpleasant. Slocum lost very little after his first night. He had spotted Gill's unconscious habit of taking a casual glance around the table just before he pulled a card from the bottom of the deck. What with Slocum's folding at this point, and Gill necessarily letting a sucker win frequently—especially with small pots—Slocum managed to stay afloat.

Gill had a broken-down cowpuncher named Danny working as a swamper. The man had fractured his spine when a bronc fell on top of him four years before. The vertebrae healed at a crooked angle. Danny's back was so twisted that it hurt all the time, and he would never be able to ride again. All he could do was mop and empty spittoons and similar undemanding work.

The first time Slocum saw Danny, the twisted little cowpuncher was moving painfully toward his table with a bucket and mop. A drunk had thrown up at the bar and Gill had snapped out, "Wake up that goddamn cripple!" Danny slept in the storeroom on a pile of old feed sacks.

When Danny showed up Gill said, "Get here faster next time, dummy."

Danny's day began at five. He mopped the entire bar and gambling area, emptied the spittoons, and carried out the empty bottles and other trash. He washed the dirty glasses and dusted the bottles in back of the bar with a feather duster. It went on for twelve hours. For this work he was paid very badly, on the grounds that he was charged nothing for sleeping on the feed sacks.

Danny said nothing to Gill's insulting remark, but Slocum immediately noticed the clenched teeth of a horseman forced to work afoot. It was hard for a man of independent spirit, like a cowpuncher, to take an insult so openly delivered. Slocum thought Danny was a potential ally.

It was one of Danny's jobs to bring drinks to the

tables for the gamblers. Sometimes he would be asked to supply fresh decks. Slocum made a point always to tip him well and say things like, "Thank you kindly," or "How are you doin' today?"

Danny began to like the man with the hard green eyes in the hard face.

Late one afternoon, before the gamblers showed up, and when the bar was quiet, Slocum sipped his beer. He suddenly said, "How'd you guys ever manage getting that Bascomb and Lloyd up those stairs?"

Bascomb and Lloyd were safe manufacturers.

"Hell, it ain't no Bascomb," Danny said. He was on his knees polishing the brass bar-rail. Henry Simpson, the day bartender, was at the other end of the bar. Gill was away somewhere.

"It's a J. J. Taylor," Danny said, pleased that he could give this information to a man he regarded as a friend. "We didn't take it up them stairs, neither. It was too big. We knocked out the winder frame in Gill's office, an' we set up a tripod hoist mebbe thirty, forty feet tall, an' we hoisted in the son of a bitch. My idee, it was. Gill didn't say a goddamn word o' thanks, neither." Slocum could see the old resentment still simmering. "Joe Gill's like a sheepherder, allus got a grouch an' a watch. When he ain't a-nursin' the one he's a-windin' the other."

"He don't pay you much, does he?"

Danny flared up. "The son of a bitch says I c'n sleep in the storeroom fer free. It don' cost him nuthin'! An' it's so small you can't cuss a cat in it without gettin' fur in your mouth. Goddamn, effen I knew the combination I'd fork that ches'nut of his'n 'n' be halfway to Colorady by sunrise. 'Cause he sure keeps a heap o' money in that thing. Other stuff, too."

"Other stuff?"

"Yeah, dokyments, I reckon."

Slocum thought they had to be negotiable bonds. He knew George Ticknor in San Francisco would give him half face value on negotiable bonds. A high charge, but when Slocum considered that Ticknor would cover Slocum's tracks so well that no one would ever be able to tie the bonds to him, the price was acceptable. He determined to look over those documents.

The J. J. Taylor, as Slocum knew from experience, needed about six tablespoons of soup. "Soup" was nitroglycerin, so called because of its thick, oily appearance. But no one handled nitro any more. It was too unstable and dangerous. Nobel had leaned how to tame that savage monster, and the result was dynamite, a very safe way to handle nitro. With a fuse and detonator, anyone could work with complete safety with dynamite. It could be stepped on, dropped, hit with a hammer, or even thrown into a fire.

What Slocum now needed was to obtain ten sticks of the stuff without arousing anyone's curiosity. Once he had them, he could go on to the next item in the agenda: cooking the dynamite till the nitroglycerin settled out of its clay housing. It was a delicate operation which had killed many of the surgeons who had tried it.

There was a turquoise mine thirty-five miles southwest of Santa Fe, near Los Cerillos. It was the closest mine to Santa Fe, Slocum knew, and where there were mines there was dynamite.

The Indians had discovered the mine hundreds of years ago. Since it produced rich blue turquoise, the color that most closely resembled the sky, from which all life came, there was great demand for it among the Zuni and Navajo.

Early the next morning, Slocum picked up his horse at the livery stable. He rode south five miles till he came to Arroyo Hondo. The arroyo headed west. Slocum rode along it to the little village of La Cienaga. He skirted its fields so that no one could get a clear impression of his passage. Five miles south he reined in. It was four o'clock in the afternoon. He examined the mine opening. A few people came in and out. Once in a while a miner wandered over to a small shack, unlocked a padlock, went in, and then emerged. The door was locked again and the miner walked over to the mine opening.

Twenty minutes later there was a dull boom. The miners had come outside for the explosion. They squatted and smoked cigarettes as they waited for the dust to settle inside.

Slocum realized that the shack was where they stored the dynamite. Satisfied, he rode on till he found a small creek that emptied into the Santa Fe River. He camped there, out of sight of the mine, and boiled some coffee. He drank from his tin cup, warming his hands as he held the cup in his palms.

It grew chilly after the sun went down. When it was dark, he stood up, leaving his roan tied to a branch of a cottonwood. It was an easy five-minute walk to the mine. No one was around the mine opening or the shack. From the window of the manager's house, four hundred feet away on the slope of a hill, came the warm glow of a kerosene lamp.

Slocum inserted the barrel of his Winchester inside the lock and twisted. The hasps pulled out with a shrill screeching noise. He waited. No one showed up. Inside, he felt around till he came to an open box. Dynamite. He helped himself to ten sticks. On a nearby shelf was some coiled fuse. He cut off two feet. Next to the fuse, and far too close to the dynamite, was a box full of detonators. He took one and rolled it very carefully in his bandanna.

Slocum was back in Santa Fe by early morning. After he had stabled his horse he dropped in at the general store on San Francisco Street. He bought the equipment he would need to extract the nitroglycerin from the dynamite, and the material to blow the safe. He bought a grey enamelled coffee pot, a bar of soap, a twelve-inch thin metal ruler, and a chunk of butter. This he bought for the waxed paper in which it was wrapped. Then he bought a bottle of Brown's elixir.

The storekeeper said, "Feelin' poorly?" as he proceeded to total the purchases.

"Back aches when I uncork the broncs on a frosty morning," Slocum said easily.

Santa Fe was six thousand feet above sea level, nestled against the Sangre de Cristo range, and the nights could get chilly. Mrs. Jenkins supplied a stove with the room, but Slocum had to pay for any wood he used. He paid ungrudgingly and, moreover, brought the wood inside himself from the cord of wood she had stacked outside. This won her respect. He had been a very quiet roomer; he had never come in drunk, nor did he try to sneak women into his room.

When he showed up with the coffee pot, she beamed. It showed, so she believed, that he intended to settle in and stay for some time. She smiled as he climbed the stairs with the old wooden box in which the general store had placed his purchases. The dynamite sticks were stuffed inside the coffee pot.

"Mr. Slocum!"

He paused and turned. "Yes, ma'am?"

"Plannin' to stay over the winter?"

"Very likely, ma'am."

"Here, let me help you." She reached for the coffee pot and grabbed it before he could stop her.

Cradling it in her arms, she accompanied him upstairs to his room. Halfway up she said, "Pretty heavy fer a coffee pot."

"I stuck the coffee beans in there, ma'am."

She was satisfied with the explanation. Slocum took the pot from her as soon as he set down the wooden box. After she left he took a handful of beans and pounded them to powder so that she would smell that aroma as he cooked out the nitroglycerin. He started a fire in the stove and set the coffee pot, half filled with water, on the stove. He waited for the water to begin simmering.

He ripped the casings from the dynamite and slid the dynamite into the boiling water, where the heat dissolved the compound. Since the nitroglycerin was heavier than the clay, it sank to the bottom.

Slocum poured off everything except the nitroglycerin into his washbasin. Then he picked up his medicine bottle and very gingerly poured the nitro into it. Nitro was immensely unstable; if a single drop were to fall on the floor it would explode like a giant firecracker, and bring Mrs. Jenkins upstairs on the double. That would be the end of his residence.

The bottle was three-quarters full by the time he had poured all the nitro into it. Next he filled it to the top with water from his pitcher. The water would prevent the nitro from sloshing around. Slocum had heard safecrackers say that a nitro bottle frequently blew up when the impact on one side of a tiny wave of soup hit the far side of the container.

He put the bottle very carefully inside his bureau drawer inside a rolled-up union suit. Then he went downstairs with the washbasin. He dumped its contents in Mrs. Jenkins's vegetable garden. The clay would improve its sandy texture and the water was always welcome.

He went upstairs, reached into his wooden box, and gingerly withdrew the detonator. This he placed in another bureau drawer, as far away as possible from the nitro. Nothing to do now except wait for a thunderstorm to come rolling out of the Sangre de Cristos.

2

Three nights later, on a Friday, Slocum played poker till midnight. He lost consistently. He bade the table good night, smiled in a friendly manner at Joe Gill as he raked in the last pot, and walked back to his room.

The low mutter of thunder in the Sangre de Cristos woke him. He got out of bed and looked up at the sky. It was black. Low clouds were racing westward. It was two o'clock, and a thunderstorm was on its way.

He dressed quickly. Everything had been ready for days. Since he wouldn't be coming back he put his extra clothes into the small valise he had bought in a pawnshop. He had placed everything necessary for the jam shot inside it. He took out the medicine bottle and packed it very carefully inside a rolled-up shirt. He stored the detonator just as carefully.

He took out a note addressed to Mrs. Jenkins, which he had written earlier. He wrote that he had just heard there was a job open in Colorado and that he regretted leaving without saying goodbye. If he got caught, Slocum reasoned, the note might confuse the jury as to his intentions and maybe he would get off with a hung jury.

At the livery stable he woke up the hostler and paid his bill, giving him the same story. He filled the saddlebags with everything except the material needed for the J. J. Taylor.

By now there were sudden sprinkles of rain. The wind was rising, beginning to blow the leaves from trees. Thunder was growling in the mountains. Occasional blue flares of lightning struck the peaks. No one was in the streets.

The lights were out in the saloon. The weather must have looked so threatening that Gill closed up early. Slocum put the roan in the alley and walked to the back of the saloon. Two trash bins were full of empty liquor bottles. A scrawny tomcat leaped from a pile of garbage and fled.

He found a rock. He took off his jacket, wrapped the rock inside the thick fabric, and broke the window in the back door. The wool absorbed most of the sound of the break-in, but the tinkle of falling glass woke Danny from his drunken sleep.

Slocum reached in a hand and slid the bolt open. He entered silently. He closed and relocked the door. He was so quiet that Danny did not hear him. He heard, instead, the angry voice of the tomcat contesting territory with another tomcat. Danny decided that the falling glass sound must have been made by the cats scrambling amid the empty bottles in the trash can. He rolled over on his dirty sacks and resumed his drunken snoring.

Slocum did not know that Danny slept in the storeroom. With the storeroom's heavy door closed, Slocum could not hear the snoring. He walked up the stairs to the second floor. He kept close to the wall, avoiding the middle of the risers where any creaking would develop.

The door to the office was locked. He had expected that, and he picked the lock within seconds.

Gill kept a bed in the office for assignations with any of the dance-hall girls he fancied. Slocum removed the ornate bedspread and draped it across the window so that no light would show. He lit his small candle and set it on top of the safe.

He listened with a pleased smile as the muttering of distant thunder became more intense.

He set everything he needed on top of the safe. The soap he had softened by fifteen minutes of hand-kneading in his room. He had wrapped it in waxed paper. He set down a lump of butter. Next he carefully set the bottle of nitro on the window ledge where he could not possibly knock it over accidentally.

Then he set down a thin metal ruler, a box of heavy wooden matches, the detonator, and, finally, his jackknife. This had been sharpened till it was as keen as a razor blade.

He picked up the ruler and inserted it lengthwise between the top of the door and the doorframe. He had first rubbed butter all over it.

He picked up the pre-worked soap and fashioned it into a cup with a funnel shape. This he pressed along the length of the ruler. He fitted it tightly. When he finished, he carefully pulled the greased ruler out.

The space the ruler had occupied provided a channel for the flow of nitro as it descended through the cup-shape.

Next, he wired the detonator. There was no point in doing the job beforehand. The powder in the center of the fuse might have jarred loose on his trip from his room.

Once lit, the flame would take six seconds before it reached the detonator.

The thunder was getting louder. It sounded like the artillery before the Battle of Chickamauga. Slocum had received one of his many scars there—a saber slash across his back, placed there by a Yankee cavalryman. The man had been fatally wounded by a shot from Slocum's carbine, yet he had had the strength to deliver a heavy slash as he fell from his saddle.

Things were coming along nicely. Next he picked up the knife which he had sharpened very carefully. He turned up the end of the fuse and slashed it twice. The second cut came at right angles to the first. He pulled the four segments apart like flower petals. It was hard to light a fuse. Usually it took four or five matches before it caught and began to sputter.

Everything was set. He took the things from the top of the safe and put them back in the valise. He pulled the mattress off the bed and dumped it on top of the safe. It would help muffle the sound of the explosion. He folded the blankets and set them in front of the safe. If it turned out to be a fine shot, the door would topple onto them.

Now came the delicate part: pouring the nitro. This process was called "drinking." In effect, he had to create a continuous chain from the bottom of the nitro, as it flowed around the edges of the door, all the way back to the detonator. If he waited too long the nitro would have drained away from the cup. All that he would get would be a crack like a .38 going off. If he shot too quickly there would be too much nitro in the cup and the door would be forced in and just about impossible to open.

He held the matches in his left hand. The nitro bottle was in his right. He had to pour, light the fuse, and do it just right. The thunder was getting closer as the storm system moved across Santa Fe. There was a rhythm. There would be a mutter, then a rumble, then three or four loud crashes.

He waited patiently.

As soon as he heard the next mutter of thunder he poured the nitro into the cup. The mutter continued for several seconds. That interval gave time for the nitro to slide along the top of the door and then along the vertical edges. Then Slocum scratched the first friction match and set the flame to the fuse. Nothing. The mutter changed to a rumble. He lit the second match. Nothing. Slocum took a deep breath and scratched the third match. This one worked. The fuse began to sputter. Slocum crouched beside the safe. A violent peal of thunder crashed just as the flame reached the detonator.

Slocum waited. Sometimes, if there had been too much nitro, the door would propel itself across the room. But this jam shot was perfect. The dull boom coincided with a massive drum-roll of thunder, and the massive door eased gently off its hinges. It toppled neatly onto the two blankets.

"Very well done," Slocum said aloud. His old teacher would have been proud of him.

He set the candle on top of the fallen door. He saw

a metal cash box twelve inches square and six inches deep. It had a lock on it. He took it out and hefted it. It was pleasantly heavy. There was nothing else in the safe. He blew out the candle and went down the stairs in the same silent way he had climbed them.

He closed the back door quietly behind him. He walked down the alley to his horse, mounted, and rode away. No one was in the street.

It had been a perfect operation, except that Danny had gone out the back door to take a leak just before Slocum had walked downstairs. With his fly open, Danny remained motionless in the shadow of the building, staring at the man who had always treated him well.

"Aw, *shit*," he said quietly. Next he noticed the broken pane in the back door.

"Well, shit," he said again. He knew he would catch holy hell from Gill. He went inside, took a bottle of bourbon from in back of the bar, and drank himself into a stupor.

It was still dark. A violent rainstorm hit when Slocum reached the Cerillos road. Protected by his saddle slicker, Slocum kept going. His horse pulled his hooves from the sticky mud with a plopping sound. Just before sunrise there was a brief flare of sheet lightning and one magnificent blast of thunder. Then a strong east wind came up and blew the clouds away. The dawn was the color of a ripe apricot. When the sun rose it poured out its warmth so intently that the ground began steaming.

A narrow creek ran into the Arroyo Hondo. As soon as there was enough light to see well, Slocum rode into a dense grove of cottonwood that edged the borders of the stream. He dismounted. No one was around for miles.

He took the cash box from the saddlebag, knocked off the small lock with the butt of his Colt, and opened the lid.

What made the box heavy was not money. Indeed, there was only fifty-seven dollars in it.

What gave it weight was a bundle of letters and various documents. The documents consisted of bills of sale and IOU's. There were plenty of stock certificates, plenty of bonds, but none were negotiable.

"Saving up for your old age, eh, Gill?" Slocum muttered. There were plenty of IOU's. Obviously these were gambling debts. Slocum always honored his gambling debts as long as he lost due to chance, and not to the kind of manipulating Gill indulged in. Slocum tore them up. "Serve you right, you bastard," he said.

Next he picked up the bundle of letters. They were in a woman's handwriting. Gill didn't look like the type who saved love letters, although, Slocum was sure, he had the kind of slick good looks some women liked.

There was nothing else to do, so Slocum began to read the letters, out of sheer boredom.

Joe Gill ran his place with a tight rein. Every Saturday morning the head bartender, a florid ex-cavalry sergeant named McNeil, had to estimate the percentage of liquor left in each bottle. The amount had to be written down. This was Gill's way of checking the amount of liquor sold each week. If the amount that had been sold out of the bottles was not matched by the cash register receipts, then either the bartenders were stealing, or the estimates were way off. In either case, McNeil got his ass reamed by Gill.

At seven in the morning Gill unlocked the front door. He wanted to check the liquor levels against McNeil's estimates before Danny started his sweeping and mopping. He slung his coat on the bar and picked up the chart McNeil had tucked into its usual place at the back of the cash drawer.

If the estimates were screwed up, which he grimly expected, McNeil was going to hear about it in rich, obscene detail. Gill reached for the first bottle on the ledge in back of the bar, Old Monongahela. This was a fine bourbon, but Gill had replaced it, once empty, with a cheap whiskey. He charged the same high price, and no one yet had complained. Slocum had discovered what was going on as soon as he had his first sip, but there had been no point in complaining, since he was interested in something much more important.

McNeil's figures were off by about thirty percent, Gill discovered. Gill was now positive that all the bartenders were linked in a plot to swindle him. His face reddened with anger.

Suddenly he became aware of a draft. His first thought was that the old drunk cowpuncher had left the back door open all night. He slammed his fist onto the bar in a fury.

He headed for the back door. As soon as he saw the broken pane of glass he realized there had been a break-in.

Gill walked around the bar carefully. Nothing seemed to be missing. All the liquor bottles seemed in place; no chairs or tables, not even any of the expensive mirrors were gone. He walked upstairs and into his office. As soon as he walked in he saw the safe door lying on the blankets.

He grinned. He never kept money in the J. J. Taylor, never more than a small amount. It was a way of telling the safecracker that he deserved something for his arduous and skillful work. He had built a hollow space between two floor joists. The almost invisible cuts in the floor were covered by the carpet.

Then he realized that the most valuable things in the safe, the letters written by Molly Hunter, were missing.

He ran down the stairs three at a time, ripped open the storeroom door, and kicked the snoring swamper in the ribs viciously.

"Wha—wha—" the startled man started to say.

Gill caught sight of the empty liquor bottle.

"Get up, you fuck," Gill said, in a hard voice full of rage. "I got a couple questions."

Gill had been doing very well at Fremont, Nebraska Territory. He had picked Molly from his stable of whores. He had recruited her in New Orleans three years before. Slocum put all of this biographical material together in his mind after he had read the letters, sitting down on the bank of the creek in the shade of the cottonwoods.

Her maiden name was Brannigan. Her father was a seaman who had abandoned her mother as soon as Molly was born. Molly was very clever and the other girls respected her and deferred to her judgment and the quick, intelligent way she settled their squabbles. So Gill picked out Molly and opened up another brothel at Ogallala, a tiny cowtown much farther west. He put her in charge of the girls. She handled her assignment with competence, and the place did very well. When the railroad workers moved on to keep pace with the advancing track, cattlemen began to patronize the place. The girls were well-behaved. Molly did not tolerate any rough stuff; when business was slow she actually rented out rooms to men who just wanted to sleep.

Then the Union Pacific chose Ogallala as a place to build a roundhouse. Now the engineers and trainmen started coming whenever they were in Ogallala. The house did so well that Gill decided not to close it down.

Every month, Molly Brannigan wrote him a detailed letter. It contained data on receipts, expenditures for doctors, bribes for the sheriff and the town marshal, food expenses for the girls, wages for the bouncer and the washerwomen and maid. After the business was taken care of she became personal. She wanted to know when he would be coming to Ogallala.

It was clear that she wanted him. Strangely for a madam, she remained faithful to the man who had first seduced her for business purposes. She went into detail about how much she longed for him. Slocum was slightly embarrassed to read such intimate details.

According to the letters, Gill visited her every three months, staying only one night. It was Slocum's firm belief that Gill had only gone to Ogallala in order to keep such a valuable asset as Molly in line.

Five years passed. Then Molly wrote that she had met a man who had spent a night in her place. Business had been slow. He was a lawyer who had come up from Santa Fe to handle some litigation involving ranch property north of Ogallala. The Bar Slash Y was suing the Three B over ownership of a small lake. This was a very important issue in dry ranch country. The trial was held in Ogallala and the lawyer had dropped in one night; someone had told him that the house was a rooming house for railroad men.

Molly Brannigan interested him very much. She was twenty-seven and the lawyer was thirty-five. He was handsome, well-groomed, and considerate. The trial was postponed. He left town and Molly thought she would never see him again.

When the trial resumed he came back, rode to her place, and asked her to marry him.

She wrote to Gill. "I am now getting close to thirty," she began. "Joe, I want my own home and children. You don't want either. I told him I would become his wife. I will stay on here till you find someone to replace me. In the meantime, wish me luck."

"Oh, not Joe Gill," Slocum said aloud. He went on reading.

"His name is John Hunter. Please, I beg you, never write to me or try to communicate with me in any way after I leave Ogallala. That was one life I had; another one begins. Please understand. *Please.*"

No wonder poor Molly Brannigan underlined the last word. She had hoped that such an appeal might work. But not with Joe Gill, it wouldn't. She signed the letter, "Molly Brannigan, soon to be Molly Hunter."

There were a few more letters. Slocum put them down and softly whistled in astonishment. John Ross Hunter was now the governor of New Mexico Territory. And the governor's office was in the old Governor's Palace—only three short blocks from Desdemona Jenkins's rooming house.

He resumed his reading, heedless of the angry blue

jay that perched on a cottonwood branch above him and scolded him.

The next letter was dated two years later. It was not signed. It said, "Your letter made me sick. I will ride out on the Canyon Road and give you the money. If anyone is on the road I will keep on going. I will return to the meeting place one hour later."

So Gill was mining poor Molly Hunter.

Two months later she wrote:

"I have no more money left in my savings account. I feel sick when I think what will happen if John asks me what happened to all that money. I will give you a diamond bracelet that he gave me two years ago. It is worth about two thousand dollars."

Slocum cursed under his breath.

A month later: "The only way I can give you more jewelry without John becoming suspicious is to go to New Orleans and have a paste imitation made. John doesn't know jewelry. I will arrange to get a letter from a good friend saying she is sick and wants me to visit. I beg you to be patient. These things take time." She added, "I had a miscarriage last week, so I will have to wait a week before I leave for New Orleans."

No wonder she had a miscarriage, Slocum thought grimly, reading on.

Then: "Please don't show John the letters! It will not be necessary! The letter came. I will leave day after tomorrow. The doctor says I will be able to travel then."

Then, two months later: "I have given you all my jewelry. There is no more. I have much trouble sleeping. John is asking me what the trouble is. I tell him it's because of the baby I lost. Thank God, that is excuse enough to satisfy him."

Slocum gritted his teeth. He tried to imagine a woman who actually was relieved that she had a miscarriage because it would serve as an excuse to an affectionate husband.

"Stinking bastard," Slocum said aloud. He had met some vile characters in his time, but blackmailers were something new in his experience.

The next letter said: "I asked John to grant a pardon to your friend Schuster, the man who is supposed to be hanged next week for killing those two cowboys in your place. He asked me why I was interested. I said it was because I used to know his mother when I lived in Ogallala. He believed me and will grant the pardon. Please don't ask me to do anything more! John will get suspicious and the whole thing will come out."

So the bastard is putting on more and more pressure, Slocum thought. *No more money, no more jewelry, now it's pardons.*

The next letter began: "Please, *please* do not go to John, I beg you. Please forget this idea about telling him that you will take my letters to the *Santa Fe Democrat*. It will kill him. Please, *please*."

Slocum stopped. He simply could not stand to read any more. The woman must have gone through torture after torture. And she could not even have the relief of telling anyone about it. No wonder Gill had put the letters in his safe. They had made him a lot of money and could make him a lot more. God only knew what the *Santa Fe Democrat* would pay to get them, or what Hunter himself would pay to prevent them from going to the paper. Gill would play one against the other and sell the letters to the highest bidder. Whatever happened, John Ross Hunter and his wife would be ruined.

In his lifetime Slocum had done plenty of unscrupulous things, but he had never done anything he considered despicable. As far as he was concerned a blackmailer was lower than any sidewinder.

Slocum took out a match and struck it. Then a thought struck him. He blew out the match. If Molly Hunter didn't know the letters had been stolen from Joe Gill—and if Joe Gill kept his mouth shut—he could still blackmail her. And she had been through enough.

The biggest favor he could do for Molly Hunter would be to ride back to Santa Fe. He would give Joe Gill's place a wide berth, go to the Governor's Palace, and put the letters in her hands. That, Slocum was convinced, would be the only way in which that tortured woman could find peace at last.

What the hell did a few more hours mean to a man with the whole West in front of him?

He mounted and rode northwards to Santa Fe.

3

"Did you let him in, you lousy cripple?"

"Wha—"

Danny could only mumble. He had been sunk deep in drunken slumber. Now Gill had viciously jerked him to a sitting position, then slapped his grey-stubbled face hard, once on each cheek.

"You broken-down fool. I asked you, did *you* let him in?"

"Let who in?"

Gill went outside in a rage, pumped a bucket full of cold water, came in again, and dumped it on top of Danny. The sudden shock sobered him. He sat up abruptly with a choking sputter.

"No call t' do that, Joe Gill," he said. "It ain't fittin' to do that."

Gill bent down. He twisted his hands into Danny's

wet shirt and pulled him close. Gill was breathing hard.

"Shut up, you asshole! Did you let him in? Yes or no?"

Danny suddenly remembered taking a piss a few hours before while it was still dark. He remembered seeing that nice stranger emerge from the back door with a cash box under his arm.

He said warily, "I din't let no one in. No sir, I—"

Gill was very perceptive. He sensed Danny's sudden caution. Something had taken place the night before; Danny had been involved. The problem was, Gill realized, that he had been asking the wrong question. He rephrased it.

"What happened last night?"

Danny liked Slocum and hated Gill, but he feared the man and he needed Gill to survive. So he said, regretting it, "I seen that new feller goin' out."

"Where were you?"

"I was takin' a piss. An' he come out with somethin' under his arm."

"What was it?"

"It was square, 'bout this here size." With shaking hands Danny sketched the dimensions of the cash box.

Gill smashed his foot on the floor in his impotent anger. "Why'n't you tell me this before?"

Danny said, in obvious surprise, "I was sleepin' one off, Joe."

Gill chewed his lip. It was obvious that Slocum thought he was going to pick up a lot of money. Instead, he found a bunch of old letters. What were the possibilities? Gill thought about them one by one.

As soon as Slocum saw that no money was involved, he might have thrown the letters away in disgust. This was what the usual robber would do. But it was Gill's feeling that Slocum was no ordinary robber. It was more likely, therefore, that he realized that if they were in Gill's safe, they had to be important. So he might have read them. Then he must have come to the conclusion that, if there was no cash in the box, he would get plenty if he tried to sell them back to Gill. But since he might figure that to be too risky, he would try to sell them to Mrs. Hunter or to the governor.

This meant that he was somewhere in Santa Fe.

"Danny!"

"Yeah?"

"Get up to the Plaza. Sit under the portal next to the Palace, mixed up with them Pueblo Indians selling their blankets."

"I don't like the way they smell—"

"Shut up. He ain't gonna notice you in that bunch. Minute you see him, run back here *fast*."

Danny sighed with relief. He still had his job and a place to sleep. He grabbed the wet feed sacks and hung them over the back yard fence on his way out to Galisteo Street. The day was cloudy and cool after last night's violent thunderstorm. The sacks would still be damp when he would finally get to them late that night. He would be coughing all the next day.

"Here! Drop this off."

Gill thrust out a telegraph blank he had filled in while Danny was in the back yard. It was an order to J. J. Taylor's Pittsburgh office for another safe.

"And get a glazier over here to fix that busted glass.

And keep your goddamned mouth shut if anyone asks any questions about the break-in."

Danny was secretly delighted at all the trouble Slocum had made for Gill. It was a pleasure for him to see Gill's money going out. On the way he stopped in San Francisco Street at the office of the *Santa Fe Herald*. He told Tom Freeman, the editor, all about the burglary. Tom promised to keep Danny's name out of it and to deny that Danny had been the source if asked. He gave Danny two dollars for the tip. That was his usual amount for any interesting news that came out of Joe Gill's place. It was Danny's way of getting even for being treated like a dog.

Slocum rode along the south side of the Plaza. Then he moved north along the east side, on Washington Street. He passed the portal where the Indians were sitting with their blankets and jewelry.

Danny arrived just after Slocum had ridden by. He hunkered down with his back against one of the pillars. The Indians gave him an incurious glance and turned aside. He had just missed catching sight of Slocum.

Slocum dismounted in front of the Governor's Palace and tied his horse to the hitching rack. He climbed the steps. The letters made a thick bundle inside the left pocket of his jacket. He hadn't shaved for three days. All his gear needed a good scrubbing and washing. Two of the governor's bodyguards had been lounging outside the front door with their arms crossed, enjoying the warmth of the sun. They straightened and stared at the dirty cowpuncher with lazy interest.

One said, loud enough for Slocum to hear, "Here

comes the new Secretary of the Treasury straight from Washin'ton, fer a fact."

The other man snickered.

There had been times in Slocum's life when he had held in his hands more money than the two of them could earn in fifty lifetimes and times when he literally didn't have a nickel to his name. The fact that he was now wearing the worn, faded gear of a working cowhand and could not afford anything else did not embarrass him.

The tall, heavy guard was named Dick Hoffman. He was former sheriff of Catron County. As soon as the Spanish majority got themselves to the polls they got rid of him; he was too vicious for their taste. He had been chewing on a matchstick. He folded his arms, stepped in front of Slocum, and said, "How come you got *that* hoss? Don' stand to reason, *amigo*."

Slocum had stolen plenty of horses in his life. But this particular roan gelding had been bought from L. R. Sims, a livestock dealer at Fort Hays, Kansas. Moreover, since he figured this sort of question would be likely to come up, he had a duly notarized and witnessed bill of sale in his saddlebag, carefully wrapped inside a square of oiled silk. He kept it there to show such obnoxious, arrogant people.

"My friend," Slocum said softly, checking the upsurge of rage that threatened his self-control, "just do what you're supposed to do. Announce me to Mrs. Hunter."

Hoffman raised his eyebrows. He took out his homemade toothpick, inspected it critically, then replaced it.

"Look here, fella," he said. "When I used t' be

sheriff down in Catron County, I ran plenty of saddle bums like you to the county line. Told 'em not to come back. Guess what?"

"They didn't come back," Slocum said, looking over the other man. This was a slender man of twenty-seven named Pete McDermott. Slocum judged him to be a Texan, based on his gear and the elaborate rowels on his spurs.

Slocum didn't much care for Texans as a group. He found them to be expert cowmen, handy with their roping, light-fingered in camp, and very fond of cards. They were a bit too brutal with their horses, quiet at work, but noisy and treacherous when they were drunk.

"Well, yes," Hoffman said, a bit surprised at the promptness of Slocum's reply. "You're absolutely goddamn right, they didn't come back."

The two men looked at each other coolly, sizing each other up.

McDermott looked at the stranger's boots with their run-down heels. McDermott had found cowboying too peaceful. He had killed two men in a drunken brawl after he had crossed the Nueces River with a big herd on its way to Wyoming, and he had just kept on going. When he rode into Catron County Hoffman recognized the Texan from a Wanted poster. Hoffman was about to go up to Santa Fe and work for the governor, and he needed another man to work with him. McDermott looked like a good bet. He was not very smart, and he was content to follow Hoffman's lead.

After his inspection of Slocum's boots, McDermott lifted his gaze a little. He next examined the left knee of Slocum's jeans. It had a neatly inserted patch. Slocum had sewn this on with the needle and thread which he always carried in his saddlebag. McDermott's gaze moved up. He scrutinized the plain steel buckle of Slocum's belt with obvious contempt.

Slocum, aware of all this, yawned. At this insolence McDermott flushed.

"I'm doin' what I'm supposed t' do," he said harshly. "I'm keepin' a broken-down raggedy-assed saddle bum from botherin' Miz Hunter. Now git!"

Slocum sat down in the chair next to McDermott. McDermott stood up. His face expressed shock and amazement at Slocum's behavior. He stood up, leaned forward, poked a finger into Slocum's chest, and opened his mouth.

"Shut up, asshole," Slocum said genially.

McDermott couldn't believe what he had just heard. He started to say something, couldn't decide what it was he wanted to say first, and finally he turned to Hoffman with a silent, pleading gesture.

Hoffman looked at his assistant in disgust. He was a strong man, slightly overweight because of the good food put out by the governor's Mexican cook. He took the match out of his mouth and carefully dropped it into a spittoon which was set on the floor just beyond the edge of a Navajo rug.

"Miz Hunter likes it real neat 'round here," he said apologetically to Slocum, who was watching with amusement the changes of expression that were sweeping over McDermott's face.

Without any warning whatsoever the big ex-sheriff swung a roundhouse open palm at Slocum. It came so quickly that Slocum was caught off-guard.

The impact knocked him sideways off the chair. By the time he had hit the floor the two bodyguards had drawn. Slocum, on his knees, looked up into the two gun barrels.

McDermott said, "Git up. Slow. No sudden moves." Slocum knew that McDermott was at his best in action. "Dick, pull his Colt an' shake out the ca'tridges."

Slocum was infuriated. He was mostly angry at himself for not being vigilant enough. He knew he was being neatly handled by two professional gunmen who would not hesitate to shoot. If they did, they knew they would be protected by the governor.

Handled. He hated the word, but it was true. He was helpless. Hoffman jerked out the Colt, swung out the cylinder, and knocked out the cartridges. Slocum toyed with the idea of tackling the skinny Texan and using him for a shield while he went after Hoffman, but he realized as quickly that the feeling was childish. If he did it, he would have every sheriff and marshal in the Territory after him for infringing upon gubernatorial dignity. They could not permit a dirty cowpuncher to profane the Governor's Palace.

Retreat here would be wise. He would find another way of seeing Mrs. Hunter. Revenge could wait.

Hoffman handed him back his empty Colt.

"Now *git!*" he said.

"What about my cartridges?"

"Your *what?* Don' give me no shit, *amigo*. I'm losin' my temper. Beat it."

"Jesus," Slocum said feelingly. "I'd sure hate to be run to the county line by you. Bet it would scare me outa my underwear. And mark me for life. Yes, sir."

Once more Slocum had underestimated his man.

Hoffman smashed him in the stomach. It was like

being kicked by a mule. He clasped his stomach in agony and bent over, gasping for breath. Hoffman kicked him. Slocum crashed into the wall. Hoffman grabbed his hair and got him into a choke hold.

"What the hell's going on here?"

Governor John Ross Hunter stood in the doorway of his office. He wore his fine linen shirt rolled up to the elbows. An expensive gold repeater watch was tucked inside his left vest pocket. A watch chain of heavy twenty-four-carat gold was looped across the vest. In the right vest pocket was a gold nugget the size of a peach pit. The chain was anchored to it.

Hoffman said, "Got a saddle bum here."

"Well, what does he want?"

"Want to see Mrs. Hunter," Slocum gasped through the brutal choke grip. He was partially paralyzed from the blow to his solar plexus. Some day, he promised himself, Hoffman would find out exactly what that felt like.

"What about?" The governor took a few steps away from his office till he was standing over Slocum.

"Answer," Hoffman said. He tightened his grip.

"Private," Slocum choked out.

"*Private?* You want to see Mrs. Hunter on a *private* matter?"

"Yeah."

"Well, damn it, what about?"

Slocum was silent. Too late he realized he should have kept his mouth shut.

"What about?" Hunter repeated. Slocum shook his head.

Hunter's right foot, clad in a very expensive, hand-made boot, reached out and prodded Slocum's hand as if it were something unpleasant and long dead. Then he turned to Hoffman and said indifferently, "Throw the bum out." He spun around and entered his office.

"You heard," Hoffman said with satisfaction. Slocum was still partially paralyzed from the hard blow to his solar plexus. The ex-sheriff nodded to McDermott. The two men bent down. Each of them locked an elbow and walked him to the door. The closer they got the faster they walked. When they reached the front door, which was open because of the warm weather, they shoved Slocum as hard as they could.

He landed on both knees. The fabric of his jeans ripped. He waited for a few seconds in that position till his muscles could function. The sun was warm and last night's rain had almost dried. It left the streets slightly muddy. McDermott went inside, picked up Slocum's dusty sombrero, and scaled it out to him. It landed in the mud near his hands. Both men laughed.

Slocum turned his head. He was still kneeling. In the midst of his laughter, McDermott suddenly realized that the icy green eyes no longer looked to be those of a saddle bum who had been summarily ejected. McDermott remembered where he had once seen a stare like that. He had been hunting in the Black Mountain Range west of Socorro, about twenty miles west of the Rio Grande. It was raining. He had just walked around a clump of quaking aspen. He almost bumped into a full-grown grizzly. As the startled, angry bear reared upright, McDermott fired. He hit the grizzly in the right shoulder. Water sprayed in the air as the heavy slug struck the wet fur. The grizzly looked down at the place of impact. Then he lowered his head and turned it sideways and looked at McDermott.

McDermott had never forgotten the power and repressed fury of that stare. The grizzly dropped to all fours and started toward him. McDermott was scared but managed to get off two accurate and well-placed shots. Because the first shot had severed the aorta, the big grizzly dropped at his feet.

And now this strange man was looking at him in the same savage, powerful way. It made him nervous, but this was a feeling he tried to conceal from himself. For a second he wished to God that the man had never showed up. He was sure it spelled bad luck.

Slocum, still on his knees, made his decision. People on the street were looking at him. There were too many witnesses, but sooner or later he knew he would run across those two. He could wait. The fury died out in his eyes. He got to his feet and picked up the sombrero. He banged it against his thigh. He ran his fingers through his hair and gave it some kind of order.

At this moment Molly Hunter looked down at the street from her third-floor window. She had looked out to gauge the weather and decide what dress she would wear. The people across the street staring at the front of the Palace attracted her attention. She looked to see what was drawing their gaze, and saw Slocum for the first time. Even from that height she could see the power of his broad back. She thought he was an unruly drunk who had just been ejected from her husband's office. Such events were not uncommon. But when he stood up she could see the man was no drunk. In spite of his unshaven face she could see the virility and power as he stood there slapping the dust from his sombrero. When he finally turned away, she wondered for a moment what it was all about. But then the anticipation of shopping filled her mind and she forgot about him.

Slocum walked away without a backward glance.

"Another day, another dollar," Hoffman said with a chuckle.

McDermott watched Slocum slide easily into his saddle. He stared after the tall man until he disappeared toward the Plaza. He felt something he had never felt before, a shiver of apprehension.

"Yeah, well, I ain't so sure," he said.

Hoffman was about to respond when the governor suddenly tore open the door of his office. He was pale. Hoffman had never seen him so disturbed. In his left hand he held two letters which had spilled from Slocum's coat when he had been knocked to the floor.

"Where'd he go?"

"Where did who go?" asked Hoffman with a puzzled look.

"God damn it, the man who wanted to see my wife! Where'd he go?"

Hoffman pointed southward.

"Get him!"

"But—"

"God damn it to hell!" Hunter yelled. "Get him and bring him back!"

Hoffman knew criminal law. "What're we gonna grab him fer? He din't do nothin'."

McDermott looked at Hoffman in contempt. He needed no excuse to shoot someone.

But Hunter had read enough to know that the rest of the letters probably packed enough political dynamite to blow him out of office. The papers, especially the one that backed the Democratic candidates,

the *Santa Fe Herald,* would give just about anything
to get hold of the letters and publish them.

"Hoffman," the governor said, restraining himself,
"ley fuga."

The old Mexican custom, the law of flight. Shoot
a prisoner in the back and claim he was shot while
attempting to escape. It was an effective way to dis-
pose of an inconvenient fellow.

"Yeah? This ain't Mexico. S'pose someone sees
us—"

"Hoffman. *Get him.*"

Hoffman shook his head slowly. He had once been
indicted by a grand jury for shooting someone in his
jail cell, and he never forgot the red tape and the
lawyer he had to pay for.

"Easy to say *'Get him,'*" Hoffman said stubbornly.

"Hoffman, you got a good job here. Want to keep
it?"

Hoffman nodded. McDermott yawned at all this
talk.

"Make sure no one sees you. Follow him till it's
safe. He's got some letters on him. They're of no
interest to anyone except me. I *want* those letters. You
can read them, I don't give a shit. But bring 'em
back."

This was a clever move, the governor reasoned. If
Hoffman was convinced that the governor didn't care
if he read them, then the chances were he wouldn't
bother. Reading was difficult for him anyway, as it
was for McDermott, who had been kicked out of school
when he was eight for fighting and had never gone
back. What else could the governor do? He couldn't
go after the man himself, and the only ones who could

do what was asked of them were these two. He had to take that chance.

The two men ran to the street. By this time Slocum was out of sight. Cursing, they ran to the back of the Palace. There was the stable with their horses. They saddled up quickly. The governor seldom got mad, but when he did things got rough. He made plenty of cutting remarks. They always took it. The pay was very good, the food and lodging that went with the job were top quality. It was the best job Hoffman had ever had, and McDermott too. Hoffman aimed to keep it as long as he could. He was also in a position to do favors for office-seekers and for people who wanted to get in to see the governor. They paid him well. Eventually Hoffman would call in the favors he had granted when the day came that the governor would lose his re-election bid.

But as of now the governor looked set for a couple more terms.

McDermott did not look ahead any further than payday. He liked Hoffman's company. The man's casual brutality appealed to him. He would follow easily where the big man led.

Danny was sitting under the portal with his back against a pillar as Slocum rode by. Danny got up unsteadily and leaned against the pillar.

"I'll be diddle-dog damned," he muttered, and began to run across the Plaza at an unsteady gait. Gill would be pleased at the information. As a result he wouldn't be kicked awake in the morning tomorrow.

By the time he reached San Francisco Street, on the south side of the Plaza, two horsemen were going

past him at a fast trot. They were Hoffman and
McDermott. Danny paid no attention.

Hunter reread the letters. He felt sick, partly because
he knew that his career would be ruined if the letters
ever got published, and partly because of the shame
he felt about marrying a whore. Everyone would be
laughing at him secretly.

He smashed his fist down on his desk in a rage.
He got up and put on his hat and coat. The conclusion
he had reached was that Joe Gill, whom he knew only
slightly, and who had contributed two hundred dollars
to Hunter's election campaign, had sent that dirty cowpuncher over to blackmail Molly. This was the first
thought that entered his mind. He decided that the
best thing to do would be drop in on Joe Gill for a
private talk.

In the meantime, Hunter thought that as soon as
Hoffman and McDermott caught up with the cowpuncher, they could be counted upon to get rid of him
and bring back the letters. When Gill found out what
had happened to his messenger and to the letters, he
would surely drop the blackmail attempt.

Danny panted. "I jus' seen 'im," he said.

Gill placed his cigar in the ashtray. He put down
the hand of poker he was holding and jerked his head.
When they were standing together out of earshot of
anyone, Gill said curtly, "Where?"

"Headin' south on Washin'ton."

Gill walked away. Two of his men, Charlie Lynn
and Harold Oakes, were eating sandwiches at a nearby
table. Gill stopped and said, "Saddle up." They grudg-

ingly rose and walked out, still chewing. Gill followed. He watched while his own horse was saddled. At the junction of San Francisco and Washington Streets, he reined in.

Lynn asked, "Where are we goin'?"

Gill waved his hand rapidly back and forth. Oakes said, "The gen'ral's thinkin', Charlie."

The horses stamped their hooves and snorted. Gill sat thinking. Slocum could have turned west and headed for Santo Domingo pueblo, or the Indian country. He could have gone east, deeper into the Sangre de Cristos and the little-traveled ranch country of the descendants of the early Spanish explorers, where strangers—if Anglos—were not made welcome. Or he could have gone south to Arroyo Hondo and thence down to Albuquerque.

He decided that the Sangre de Cristos was the most unlikely route. That left two. He took out a silver dollar and spun it. It came down tails.

"O.K., west," Gill said. They moved off at a fast trot.

Governor Hunter was in a fever of impatience. He paced back and forth across his office. He went to one wall, on which there hung portraits of the former governors. Then he walked back again to the opposite wall. That held a six-by-six-foot map of New Mexico. He stopped and moved close to it, drew a circle around Santa Fe with his forefinger.

"You're somewhere in there, you son of a bitch," he muttered.

Molly Hunter said in an amused tone, "Talking to yourself?"

Hunter could not look at her. He kept his gaze locked on the map. "Looking for someone, Molly." His voice was tense and jittery. "Someone in there." He banged his fist against the map in a sudden up-welling of anger.

He thought with annoyed pleasure that she was still beautiful. Her copper-red hair fell in a thick mane to her shoulders. She was almost as tall as he was. Her skin was the color of cream. She had high, firm breasts and brown eyes. She wore a simple green dress that clung to her body.

She came up behind him and put her arms around his waist, patted his stomach fondly, and said, "You're eating too much, John."

He pulled her arms away abruptly. She stared at him. Her arms hung by her side.

"I've been busy," he said shortly. "Very busy." He did not look at her. She kept staring at him. This kind of behavior was not like him at all. After a few seconds she turned and walked thoughtfully out of his office. He dug his nails into his palms in an effort to control himself. The first person he wanted to kill was the cowpuncher who had come in with the letters; the second would be Joe Gill. And the third would be the former whore who was now Molly Hunter.

Slocum's anger simmered down as he rode south. Perhaps it would be wiser not to go after those two bodyguards. The entire power of the Territory would fall on him if he did. The result would be that he would have to stay away from New Mexico for a long time, at least until there was a new governor. That was possible, seeing that the opposing newspaper would be pushing any other candidate as an alternative to Hunter.

But in the meantime, what could he do about the letters?

Slocum pondered his choices.

He could burn them and let Molly Hunter know what he had done. He rejected that idea almost as soon as he had made it, because she would never be sure whether he was telling the truth.

No, he had to hand her the letters. A woman whose life had been a private hell for the last five years, who had lost her baby as a result, certainly deserved kind treatment. Slocum knew he was the only man who could give her the peace of mind she was in such desperate need of.

He riffled through the letters. It was then that he discovered that two of them were missing. "Damn," he muttered. They must have fallen out of the bundle when he had been fighting with Hunter's bodyguard. It followed that the governor had seen them, and probably thought Slocum was the blackmailer, or the blackmailer's representative.

Slocum came to an abrupt halt. He wondered what the governor would do now. First of all, Slocum guessed, Hunter would want to confront his wife and beat her. But, since a governor's lady with blackened eyes and a broken nose would have a poor effect on the next campaign for re-election, which was coming up in three months, he wouldn't lay a hand on her. But she'd hear about it.

If the governor were wise, he would come to the decision—if he loved his wife—that whatever his wife had done before her marriage, she was someone else now.

Slocum asked himself what he would do in this situation if he were the governor. He decided that he simply did not know. But one thing was sure: he'd try like hell to get the rest of the letters. He'd kill the man who was carrying them as well as Joe Gill. Better to kill the blackmailer and his agent and then go to prison, rather than be drained of money and peace year after year. And, since juries hated blackmailers, there was a very good chance that the grand jury would decide it was justifiable homicide and refuse to bring an indictment. Even if indicted, there was also a very good chance that he would be found not guilty.

The conclusion that Slocum came to was this: the two bodyguards were probably riding after him right this second with no intention of bringing him back alive, as long as they had the letters.

"Oh, Christ," Slocum said. What he should do was to keep on going till he was out of the Territory, and forget the whole damn thing. True, it was Joe Gill who had cheated at poker; in exchange, Slocum had blown his safe and retrieved the letters. Call it quits.

With a start Slocum suddenly realized that Joe Gill himself would be after him as well, and for exactly the same reason and motivation that Hunter had: kill Slocum and get the letters.

"I'm certainly a popular feller 'round these parts," Slocum said aloud with a slow grin. The situation had its comical side. It was even more reason to head for high ground. On the other hand, he thought, if he were to head back to Santa Fe and the governor's lady, all of them would be surprised. They would never believe that he would stick around town, what with two sets of killers searching for him.

He swung his horse's head around. But before he

went to Santa Fe he would ride deep into the Sangre de Cristos and look up Candelario Borrego, of Mesa Borrego. He needed someone to work with now, and Candelario was a man he could trust.

4

While Slocum rode north along the Rio Gallina, he worked out the problems he was facing. It would clearly be difficult to reach Molly Hunter. The two bodyguards were no fools; they would probably notify their friends around town to pass on any information about him being in Santa Fe. And if Slocum succeeded in getting close to her, one or both of them would spot him.

What he needed was a trusted messenger, someone who could get to Molly Hunter without drawing attention to himself. And the only person he could think of who was reliable, who could get away with it because of his intelligence and his ability to blend in with the dominant Latin population, was Candelario Borrego.

Candelario lived on the Mesa Borrego, an isolated flat-topped mountain set in the very center of the wild jumble of mountains that formed the heart of the San-gre de Cristo range.

Four years before, Slocum had been running a wholesale grain and feed operation in Taos. Its sole purpose was as a cover for a large-scale rustling scheme, since he dealt in cattle as a normal accompaniment to his regular business.

One of his trusted employees was Candelario. Candelario's ancestors had wormed their way up the narrow, twisting canyon of the Rio Gallina hundreds of years before. They were searching for good grazing land for their cattle and a place far from the arm of the Viceroy in Mexico City. Moving slowly among deep canyons and eight-thousand-foot peaks, they suddenly came upon the wide and beautiful mesa topped with rich grasslands. It was beautiful and lonely. It was promptly christened Mesa Borrego. Later on, others rode north to New Mexico. On the easy slopes bordering the Sangre de Cristos on the west was the Santo Domingo de Cundiyo grant. The owners of the grant kept strangers from riding across their land, so the only open approach to Mesa Borrego was kept closed by the grant. That increased the Mesa Borrego's isolation. Candelario liked it that way.

Three years before, Slocum had loaned two hundred dollars to Candelario. He said he needed it to start building barbed-wire fences to do some intelligent breeding of his stock. Slocum loaned him the money without hesitation. A year later Octavio, Candelario's son, who was in his mid-twenties, rode into Taos with a note from Candelario asking for another two hundred to finish up the fencing. Slocum gladly gave the money to Octavio, who struck him as a rather sullen youth. There had been no word since, and Slocum assumed it was because Candelario still hadn't been able to sell off his stock yet. These people had trouble writing, but they had long memories, so Slocum did not worry.

Now it was time to collect. If Candelario did not have the money, Slocum would ask him for a couple of days of his time, plus his intelligence, and that would wipe out most of the debt.

It was a thirty-five-mile ride along the twisting trail that edged itself along the winding Gallina Canyon. Then another such horse track went east for eight miles across savagely broken mountain country: canyons, barrancas, arroyos. There was never enough flat grassland to graze cattle. That was why most of the people looking for land bypassed this area. A man might keep sheep or goats here. Slocum rode on. He followed the contour lines; that was the easiest way to travel. Then he rounded a bend and saw the rich, grassy mesa. Adobe houses were scattered across it. Each had its neat woodpile. Goats looked at him with their cynical yellow stare. Children stared at him, their mouths open in astonishment at seeing a stranger.

He halted in front of a goatherd of eight and said in Spanish, "Where is the house of Candelario Borrego, my son?"

The boy's mouth remained open. He was very shy. Slocum repeated the question.

Finally he pointed in the Mexican way, using his outthrust chin. "There is the house of the Borregos, *señor.*"

As Slocum approached the house a haggard woman emerged and folded her arms. The screaming of the excited children had alerted her that a stranger was approaching. People everywhere stopped what they were doing to watch.

"Buenas tardes, señora."

"Buenas tardes, señor."

"I came to speak to your husband, *señora.*"

"He died a year ago, *señor.*" Her face was impassive.

The news came as a shock. "My regrets, *señora.* He was an old friend." But Candelario had left a son, and the son was responsible for the father's debts.

"May I speak to your son? We have business to discuss."

"He is in the village. Are you *Señor* John Slocum?"

"I am, *señora.* You pronounce my name in the American Style."

"Yes. Candelario often spoke of you and your kindness."

She said to one of the children, "Bring Octavio." The boy ran off.

"I knew you would come some day, *señor.* And so one's deeds are paid for."

Slocum did not understand, and said so.

She said, "When my husband was still alive, Octavio had honor. Now he has none."

Slocum waited patiently.

Octavio appeared. From the slow, almost indolent way he approached, it was clear that he wanted to postpone this meeting as long as possible. He slouched against the wall, looking everywhere but at Slocum.

"Octavio," Slocum said, with a hard, patient tone, "since you have not come to see me with the money your father owed, I have been forced to come to you. Why have I not seen you in Taos?"

Octavio mumbled, "My father died. I was unable to pay your honor."

"Can you pay me now?"

"No. I, Octavio, I have nothing."

"Do you know how much you owe me?"

"Not exactly, your honor."

"Four hundred dollars."

"Aii," his mother said under her breath.

"It is so, since your honor says it is so."

"Can you not pay me at least a part of it?"

Slocum fervently hoped that Octavio would not be able to.

"I have nothing."

Slocum was secretly delighted, but he put on a look of severe annoyance.

"Then you must come with me and work for me."

"I am ready," Octavio said. "I believe your honor's demand is just."

"Then get ready."

"I am ready. I wear all I possess."

His mother began to cry. "Your honor claims your right," she said. "But how miserable I am in my old age! He is my only child. But he has not followed his father's example. But will the gentleman not dismount and enter my poor house?"

Slocum yielded. As he walked inside, he said gently, "Your husband was a worthy man. How has his son fallen into so miserable a position?"

"Ah, señor, he has gambled away everything."

Slocum sipped the goat's milk she set in front of him. He said, "I would not have given him the money but for the letter from his father, señora. How could he recommend that I give the money to a son whose character he must have known?"

"Ah, señor, my husband never wrote that letter; my boy forged it."

Slocum's face darkened with anger. "Then it is

right he should be punished," he said. And you, *señora*, must comfort yourself. As the boy is now, he can never give you any help. I will take charge of him. I will teach him how to work and how to live like a respectable man. And so the time will come when he will return to you an estimable character."

He turned to Octavio and said curtly, "You will come with me to Taos."

"As your honor pleases," Octavio said, flushing.

While Octavio saddled his horse his mother prepared tortillas and stewed goat meat for them to take with them. Slocum rode ahead so that their leave-taking could be private. After a few minutes Octavio caught up with him. He was silent, and his eyes were red-rimmed. He looked at Slocum resentfully and ran his sleeve across his dripping nose.

After half an hour of silence he said abruptly, "What will I do for you in Taos?"

The kid was behaving normally, Slocum noticed. He had dropped the respectful "your honor" and was down to "you." Slocum repressed a smile. This showed signs of spirit. He would have need of that.

"We are not going to Taos," he told the boy.

Octavio reined in abruptly. "I will not go with you elsewhere!" he shouted. "It is only to Taos that I will go!"

"Why?" Slocum asked gently.

"Elsewhere is too far!"

"We are going to Santa Fe. This is not the edge of the world."

"No! I will not—"

"Or I will take your forged letter to the sheriff."

Octavio clenched his teeth in silent anguish. It suddenly struck Slocum that he was now indulging in blackmail.

"Well?" he asked, amused at the irony of the situation.

Octavio dropped his eyes and looked at his saddle-horn. "Yes," he whispered. "All right."

"Let me hear no more talk," Slocum said harshly. "You will work for me briefly. If your work is satisfactory, I will release you from all your obligations and burn your forgery in front of you. Then you will be free to return home, and I hope you will have learned something. You will have a delicate and dangerous task to perform."

"With your permission, *señor*, I do not understand."

Slocum told him.

Octavio thought it over for a minute. Then he burst out, "But the wife of the governor!"

Slocum reined in. They were sitting their horses beside the narrow Santa Fe River, where it flowed out of the Sangre de Cristo range.

"It will be difficult, yes," Slocum said. His horse stretched its neck to drink. "Probably her husband is having her watched because he thinks I will make another attempt to see her. He knows what I look like. So does the bodyguard. So you must pick your time carefully. And when you manage to talk to her, tell her I am here. Tell her to come by alone. If she wants to know why you don't have the letters with you, tell her I don't want them intercepted. *Claro?*"

"*Claro,*" Octavio said. He was not happy. Then he asked, "What is so important about these letters?"

Slocum should have told him it was none of his

business, but he was so tired from the days of endless riding that his mind did not work properly.

"They were written when she was young and in love. She would not like her husband to read them."

"How much is she paying you for them?" Octavio's eyes narrowed at the thought of their possible value.

"Nothing."

"Nothing?"

Slocum realized that there was no point explaining his motivations to someone like Octavio. "Just be careful, Octavio," Slocum said. "I would not like to tell your mother that you were, unfortunately, shot."

"Shot?"

"Do it, Octavio, then come back here. Or I will do what I promised." Slocum was getting sick of this kid. *"Claro?"*

"Claro," Octavio muttered.

Slocum watched him ride away along the willow-fringed river. He didn't like the boy's sullen attitude. But then he remembered that an old miner once told him, "A broken shovel's better than none at all." There was no one in the area who was under any obligation to Slocum except this particular broken shovel.

Slocum dismounted. He put the letters onto his spread-out saddle slicker and rolled it up tightly. He found an old rotten log fifteen feet away. He rolled the log to one side, set the slicker down, and rolled the log back. He scrutinized the area. No one could tell that the log had been moved. He pulled the saddle off, draped the sweaty saddle blanket over a horizontal branch of a nearby willow to dry it. He drove a picket-pin into the ground, tied his riata to it, and let the horse graze on the grass beside the road. He leaned back against the saddle, tipped his sombrero over his eyes, and fell immediately into an exhausted sleep. He thought Octavio should be back before dusk.

As he rode along Canyon Road, Octavio was thinking hard. If he stood any chance of being intercepted by the governor's bodyguard he stood a good chance, he felt, of being beaten or even shot.

What for? he asked himself. To pay off his father's debt? Nonsense! As for the forged letter he had written, how did he know that Slocum would keep his word about dropping the whole matter? Octavio knew what he would do if the situation were reversed: he would keep the letter and force Slocum to do his bidding for the rest of his life. That was what an intelligent man would do, Octavio decided. And Slocum was clearly intelligent.

Octavio did not trust anyone. And so he came to a conclusion that he considered brilliant. He would blackmail Molly Hunter—which he was positive Slocum was doing—and he would tell the bodyguard where they would find Slocum. Slocum had said they were killers. When Slocum refused to tell them where the letters were, they would torture him, then kill him. And the best part of it was that the letters would be in Octavio's possession. He would go to Santa Fe and look over the lay of the land, get a look at the governor's wife, take a look at the bodyguard. Then he would ride back very quietly. Sometime during the night Slocum would be asleep. He had been exhausted on the ride down from Mesa Borrego. He would have to fall asleep eventually. Octavio had learned the trick of stalking people from the Pueblo Indian children he ran across when he was herding goats long ago. Octavio was good at it; he could come so close to a deer that he could actually touch it.

He would leave his horse a mile away and stalk Slocum. The letters were in Slocum's saddlebags. He would take them out and hide them in a good place near the road between there and Santa Fe. Then he would ride back and tell the bodyguard where Slocum was. The bodyguard would ride out.

He could not find a thing wrong with this plan. He began to laugh as he rode toward Santa Fe.

Octavio was in too much of a hurry. He sat his horse a hundred yards from the Governor's Palace. He was waiting to see Molly Hunter emerge. McDermott was the first man to notice.

"Dick," he said, as he stood at the window munching an apple.

"Yeah?"

"Some greaser's been across the street for a couple of hours. All he does is look at the front door."

"Don' worry about it. He's prob'ly got a petition. Ever since they had all this trouble about land grants they all got petitions."

"How come he don't jus' step in?" McDermott asked.

"He's prob'ly from the Rio Chimayo country. They git pretty shy around Anglos."

McDermott was not convinced. Twenty minutes later, he knew he was right. Molly Hunter walked down the front steps to do some shopping. He watched her rich, full bottom strain and tighten against the green silk of her dress. He sighed and went on with his apple. He turned and idly took a look at the unknown man on horseback.

That person suddenly sat upright as he recognized the red-headed woman Slocum had mentioned. As he slowly began to ride after her Hoffman said, "Yeah, Pete. Guess you're right. Find out what the critter's up to."

McDermott went down the steps and tossed away his half-eaten apple. He intercepted Octavio's horse just past the Governor's Palace. He grabbed the bit with his left hand and jerked hard. The horse's head was pulled savagely to its right. It came to an abrupt halt.

Octavio yelled, *"Que pasa, hombre?"*

McDermott's .45 was pointing at his head. Octavio subsided to a nervous mutter as he realized that this man, who had come out of the same house she had emerged from, must be one of the bodyguards.

"Abajo," McDermott said. Octavio dismounted. McDermott jerked the muzzle in silence toward the side door of the Palace. Octavio moved reluctantly. He thought that he should have stayed much farther away, probably on foot. This was a hard man; he had a quality missing in Slocum, who was also hard. The quality, which Octavio lacked words to define, was one of mindless viciousness. Octavio was scared. McDermott followed. Octavio's horse followed at the end of the reins. When Octavio climbed the steps to the side door, it opened just before he got there.

"Pase," Hoffman said. He reached out and grabbed a fistful of Octavio's old shirt, ripping it. Then he forced Octavio to his knees. McDermott hitched his horse to the rack and then stood in back of Octavio.

"Arriba!" Hoffman snapped. He jerked Octavio erect, ripping the shirt even more. It was a routine they had worked out to use on prisoners. McDermott kicked hard. Octavio sprawled flat; it was obvious to Hoffman that the boy was terrified. He concealed his smile.

"Arriba, hombre, arriba!" yelled Hoffman. Octavio now felt that he was in the presence of two vicious, unpredictable men. This would not have worked with Slocum, but it was effective with nearly everyone else.

Hoffman walked to the door, closed it, and locked it so that the prisoner would feel even more closed off from the outside world. Then he turned around and kicked Octavio with casual boredom until he fetched up in a corner.

McDermott bent down. Hoffman said warningly, "Pete! Knife."

McDermott searched the recumbent, terrified Octavio. He ripped open his shirt and looked for an underarm sheath. Not finding it, he squeezed the pants pockets. Next he ripped off both badly worn boots and looked inside them for a secret sheath.

Satisfied, he stepped backward. Hoffman then bent down and asked gently, *"Habla ingles?"*

"Sí," said the grateful Octavio, sensing that now the beating and yelling was over, *"Sí!"*

"That's good." Without a second's hesitation, Hoffman smashed his big right fist into Octavio's mouth. The startled man spat out broken teeth.

"Now that I got your attention," Hoffman said genially, "you tell me why you're follerin' Miz Hunter."

"I no follow nobody. I—" Octavio had planned

to say that he was just sightseeing around Santa Fe. He would have told them this with a wide-eyed, friendly smile, he planned, and then they would have let him go. But things were not working out that way at all.

Hoffman kicked Octavio in the ribs. Octavio sucked in his breath in agony and clamped his hands over the place of impact. By the grating sensation under the skin, he knew that one, maybe even two ribs had been broken. He sat up and edged himself painfully against the wall at his back.

"What's that you said?" Hoffman asked with the smile Octavio had come to dread.

"I no—"

McDermott's pointed boot toe kicked him in the testicles. He rolled up in a ball with his hand between his legs, holding his scrotum. Tears welled from his eyes. McDermott watched with pleased interest.

Hoffman said, "Once more. Why you follerin' 'er?"

He drew back a foot. Octavio held up a hand to ward off the expected kick.

He gasped out everything.

Back at the temporary camp, Slocum had drawn up his knees. His head rested on them, his arms were clasped around his legs, and his sombrero was tilted over his eyes. He slept deeply. It was the deathlike sleep of extreme exhaustion.

Since McDermott and Hoffman had beaten Slocum's exact position from Octavio, they were able to come up to him quietly.

Suddenly his Colt was dragged from its holster. By the time he jerked awake, McDermott had smashed the butt of his Colt across the right side of his head.

The only thing that saved Slocum from a bad fracture was the fact that the felt of the sombrero cushioned the blow.

Slocum sprawled flat in a daze. Through the pain and his semiconscious state he was aware that he was being dragged to his horse. Dim figures grabbed his saddle blanket and saddle. The latter was cinched into position. Then he was suddenly hoisted roughly across the saddle. His feet were on one side, his head and shoulders on the other. He was still so weak and dizzy that there was nothing he could do. McDermott unhitched Slocum's riata. With it he lashed Slocum's ankles to the left stirrup. Then he threw the riata under the horse, walked to the other side, and tied Slocum's wrists firmly to the right stirrup. He coiled the rest of the line on the horn.

"They in the saddlebags?" he asked Hoffman.

"No, they ain't!"

Slocum was fully conscious by now. He kept his eyes closed.

"The greaser said they was."

"Well, god damn it, they ain't! Stop talkin' like an old woman!"

"So where are they?" McDermott said stubbornly.

"Well, they's somewhere else, ain't they?" Hoffman said with heavy sarcasm. "He knows where. Let's ask 'im."

"O.K." McDermott walked over to Slocum's head and slapped his face hard.

"Jesus," Hoffman said. "Not *here*. Ain't you got *any* brains?" There had been complaints about prisoners being questioned by the two of them in public.

Slocum lifted his head.

"Look!" McDermott jeered. "He jus' woke up from his beauty sleep."

Hoffman dropped back and looked critically at Slocum. He had made a study of how long people held out before they caved in. Octavio's willingness to talk after exactly one minute was no surprise, but something told Hoffman that this was no one-minute job, or even a five-minute job. Maybe never. The right side of Slocum's head was soaked in blood from the long gash McDermott's gun butt had opened. Horseflies kept buzzing around the blood, and occasionally lighting on his bloody hair.

Slocum turned his head sideways and up. The moon had risen over the Sangre de Cristos, and its light was pouring into the valley of the Santa Fe River.

Hoffman felt a bit uneasy as he looked at that harsh, unyielding green stare.

"Wanna tell me where you put them letters, *amigo?*" he asked genially.

"What letters?" Slocum said. His head felt as if someone were banging it against a cobblestone.

Hoffman smiled. "We're gonna start talkin' 'bout 'em soon. In private. Thought you might wanna think it over an' remember where you put 'em. So think it over a bit. Mebbe your memory will get better."

Slocum vomited. McDermott said, "Shit," and kicked his horse away. Slocum realized the blow had hurt him worse than he thought. Perhaps he had a concussion. Vomiting was one of the signs of that.

McDermott reached down and grabbed Slocum's hair and pulled his head around.

"Listen," he said, "I don' mind you got trouble rememberin'." His smile was cold. "I'm gonna enjoy proddin' your memory."

As they rode along the east side of the Plaza they passed Danny. He had been carrying a sack of sawdust from the lumber mill back to the saloon. Danny stared at Slocum's bloody head. Then he suddenly recognized Slocum. He started to walk faster in his haste to report to Joe Gill.

5

"Stable'd be better," Governor Hunter said. Hoffman, with his hand on the doorknob, looked at him curiously.

"Molly might hear him," Hunter said in explanation.

Hoffman grinned. McDermott muttered, "Shit," under his breath.

Hunter turned toward him. "Say anything?" he asked coldly.

"He din't say nuthin'," Hoffman said promptly. He knew about McDermott's explosive temper and sought to defuse it. He turned toward McDermott and said warningly, "Right, Pete?"

"Yeah. Din't say nuthin'."

McDermott led Slocum's fine horse into the stable and undid the riata. He coiled it and hung it over the horn. Slocum was still dizzy and weak. McDermott casually flipped his legs up in the air with as much boredom as if Slocum were a sack of wheat. Slocum slid head downwards and landed with a heavy, painful thump onto the stable floor. The blow started the bleeding again.

"Not a bad hoss you got there," Hoffman said critically. He unsaddled it and led it into one of the empty stalls.

Slocum slowly sat erect. He held his throbbing, bleeding head in his hands. Hunter walked out. McDermott had been waiting for that. He jerked Slocum to his feet and pulled him toward one of the upright oak beams that supported the roof. He placed his open palm on the back of Slocum's head and suddenly slammed Slocum face first against the beam. Slocum had just time enough to turn his head slightly. He avoided a broken nose, but the impact opened his left cheek to the bone.

McDermott was ready with a length of rawhide. He tied Slocum's wrists together as tightly as he could. When he was finished he nodded to Hoffman.

"I'm gonna ask you a question, cowboy. One question. Now, before I ask, I'm gonna demonstrate somethin'. Pete, drag in the demonstration."

McDermott grinned. He walked to the end stall, bent down and grabbed what appeared to Slocum to be a brown sack. He dragged it in front of Slocum and let it drop.

It was Octavio. His clothes were a bloody mess. McDermott said, "Shit," with a disgusted tone and wiped his bloody hand on a bunch of hay. Octavio's face was an indescribable mess. The nose was broken and pushed to one side; one cheekbone was broken and both eyes were swollen shut. His front teeth were snapped off at their roots.

"He tol' us where you was," Hoffman said cheerfully. "But he was so quick about it I figgered he was layin' a false trail. So I talked to 'im some more. An' he kept tellin' the same story. So we rode out an' there you was, jus' where he said. A nice li'l ol' truth-teller, that greaser. Friend of yours, he said."

Hoffman prodded the moaning, soft mass with his toe.

"So the son of a bitch was tellin' the truth all the time. It jus' goes to show you, don' it? Sorta looks like he wintered on pine cones, don' he?" He looked critically at Octavio.

So Octavio had betrayed him, Slocum thought, without anger. The boy had paid for his treason. Slocum sighed. He had calculated badly. He should have known that a man who gambled and forged letters could not be trusted.

Hoffman was talking. Slocum listened. "Now, what me an' the governor want to know is this: where'd you put them letters? We know who sent you, we jus' want them letters. *All* of 'em. I'll give you a minute to answer. An' while you're thinkin' it over, keep lookin' at the greaser. It might help you to remember."

Without any warning, Hoffman sunk his right fist into Slocum's right kidney. Slocum let out a grunt of pain.

"That's to help your mem'ry," Hoffman said with a pleased grin. He stepped back and walked around the upright beam. He stood facing Slocum. "All right, Pete," he said. Then he folded his arms and waited.

Slocum could now see McDermott's face. He was

standing slightly to one side of Hoffman and in back of him. A muscle twitched in his left cheek. His eyes were bright. It came as no surprise to Slocum that the slender Texan enjoyed inflicting pain.

"Minute's up," Hoffman said. He waited five more seconds, till a look at Slocum's face made it crystal clear that the man would keep silence.

"All right, Pete," he said.

McDermott took a swift stride toward Slocum as if he were a hunting dog whose owner had just left him off his leash. A quirt hung from his wrist by its loop.

He slid around to Slocum's rear. He reached out with both hands, gripped the shirt collar, and suddenly ripped it down to the waist. He lifted his arm. The quirt loop slid down into his hand. He slashed the braided rawhide across Slocum's back. A thick red welt appeared on his lower back. At the sound of the impact, Octavio whimpered. He rolled himself into an even tighter ball.

Slocum did not flinch. He said, "You did a pretty good job on the kid. Bet you had a good war record, burned houses, raped a few old ladies, got yourselves a couple medals."

Hoffman had been a sergeant with the Fifth Ohio Volunteers. He did not care for the remark.

"He's got a big mouth," he said.

"I'll make it smaller," McDermott said. He swung the quirt viciously across Slocum's face. Red welts appeared on both cheeks. Octavio moaned.

"It's gonna git worse," Hoffman said. "Believe me, *amigo.*"

Slocum slowly turned his head and stared at the ex-sheriff. The green eyes burned. The face was impassive. Suddenly Hoffman felt uneasy. When McDermott lifted the quirt again Hoffman felt his heart beat quicker. He was sure now that Slocum would never talk.

"Hold it," he said.

McDermott reluctantly lowered his quirt. Hoffman took him by his elbow and led him out of earshot. McDermott leaned against the stable wall while he nervously flicked his quirt at his dusty boots.

"Well?" he demanded.

"It's not gonna work, Pete."

"Oh, yes it will!"

"Not with that quirt. It don't hurt enough. I got a better idea. Get a riata." They walked back. McDermott went inside the tack room at the end of the stable and found a riata hanging on a peg. When he came out with it Hoffman said, "Throw one end over that overhead beam."

When the riata was hanging Hoffman said, "Now help me tie his hands in back of 'im."

"What the hell fer?"

"We're gonna tie his hands in back of 'im. I'm gettin' sick of givin' you an affydavit ev'ry time I move, Pete."

Slocum thought when they untied him the perfect time would come to make a break for the nearest Colt in their gunbelts. A tiny smile appeared on his lips.

Hoffman was very observant. Without a word of warning he smashed the gun barrel against Slocum's head. It landed on top of the old wound and reopened the scab that had formed.

He was dazed. Hoffman said crisply, "O.K., fast." McDermott quickly removed the rawhide strip that held Slocum's hands around the upright beam. Slocum, dizzy with the impact of the blow, slid to his knees. McDermott immediately lashed his wrists together at his rear.

Hoffman then tied one end of the suspended riata hanging down from the roof beam. Then he hoisted. Slocum's arms, pinioned at his rear, went up. When they had reached the limit of travel dictated by the structure of the upper arms and shoulder blades, his shoulder joints locked. Hoffman kept hauling on the riata until Slocum's toes just touched the ground. McDermott shoved Slocum with the palm of his hand and set Slocum swinging back and forth. His boot toes swept back and forth across the dusty ground.

The agonizing strain at his shoulders jarred Slocum to full consciousness.

"Well, now, *amigo*," Hoffman said cheerfully. "Here we are again. Feel like talkin' yet?"

Slowly and deliberately, Slocum shook his head.

Hoffman stepped back and nodded at McDermott.

McDermott put all his strength into a powerful overhand swing of the quirt. Even Hoffman winced at the dull *thock!* of the braided rawhide. Slocum's back muscles jumped under the blow, yet Slocum's face remained impassive. McDermott lifted the quirt once more. Slocum turned his head sideways and held his gaze steady on Hoffman's face as the quirt whistled down.

Hoffman waited with growing irritation. Slocum made no sound. Hoffman nodded slowly, as if he were answering a question he had just put to himself. He took McDermott's elbow once more and pushed him outside the stable.

"Pete," he began.

"He'll talk!" McDermott's face was flushed. "They allus talk!"

"Not this one," Hoffman said. "Not with whippin'. So I'm gonna leave 'im hang there all night. It gits worse, jus' hangin'. Gag 'im so's he won't yell. You'll see, come mornin' we won't have no problems coaxin'. None at all, Pete." Hoffman wasn't sure of that last statement, but it never did for McDermott to find out that he, Hoffman, had doubts.

As Pete looked for an old rag, Hoffman went on, "I'm gonna eat somethin' in the kitchen. I ain't et all day."

"All right, Dick," McDermott said reluctantly. "Tell Juanita to fry me a steak 'n' eggs. I'll be right in. Guess you know your business."

"I do, Pete, I do," Hoffman said gently.

Molly Hunter watched from her bedroom window while the two men closed the stable door. It was a warm night. The window was open and she heard Hoffman say, "What about the greaser?"

McDermott responded, "He's hurt too bad to wander around, Dick."

She waited until they were in the kitchen. Her curiosity had been aroused by the sound of the quirt striking flesh, and that last remark of McDermott's made her feel sick. She heard them sitting down at the kitchen table. When the sound of the clatter of dishes came she put on a long coat and went downstairs quietly. They did not see her go by.

She opened the stable door and then closed it quietly. The first thing she saw was Slocum as he hung from the beam. Blood had clotted on the right side of his head. His right cheek had been split open, and a trickle of blood still oozed from the length of the cut. The welts on his face and back had puffed up.

She stepped close. Molly Hunter had seen plenty in her years on the frontier, but this was pretty bad.

Slocum did not look up. He thought that either Hoffman or McDermott had come back to see if he were ready to talk. Then he suddenly smelled perfume and he lifted his head.

Later, she remembered that the thing that surprised her the most was the calm harshness of the green eyes.

"Who are you?" she whispered.

"John Slocum. I bet you're Molly Hunter."

"Why are they beating you?"

Slocum lifted his head with an effort. She was very angry, and controlling herself was clearly difficult.

"I got the letters you wrote to Joe Gill."

Her face went white. She stepped back and said in fury, "You son of a bitch! You stole 'em from him and now you're figgerin' on some of that easy money for yourself!"

"Stole 'em, yeah. But I was trying to give 'em back to you."

"Lyin' bastard! Serves you right! I hope they kill you!" She turned to go.

"Mrs. Hunter."

His voice surprised her with its air of calm command. Against her will, she stopped and turned again.

"I blew Joe Gill's safe. No money in it, but I didn't know that. I took a box thinking it was money, but when I opened it all I found inside were the letters."

"He's telling everyone that the damn fool who did it didn't find any money."

"Yeah. So I read the letters."

She flushed. "Enjoy 'em? Thought you'd make some money too?"

"That's not what I do for a living," Slocum said quietly.

There was something so direct and convincing about that statement that she fell quiet.

"When I finished reading the letters I said to myself, 'Joe Gill didn't lose any money, so he must be feeling pretty good about that. But then he must be awful mad about losing those letters.' So I said, 'How can I get him so mad he'll just go and bite himself to death like the goddamn rattler he is? Why,' I thought, 'just go and give the letters back to the lady who wrote 'em, no charge.'"

"Why do you hate Joe Gill so much?"

"The son of a bitch plays poker with a marked deck."

"He always did. So you blew the safe to get even?"

"Hurts him worse than being shot."

Slocum's mind was working fast. They were spending a lot of time talking and if the two men came back suddenly . . . He had to persuade her to untie him and let him go. It would be his only chance.

She stood there thinking.

"But I still don't understand why they're beating you—oh, my God!" She had caught sight of Octavio.

"They did *that?*" Her face was pale.

"They thought he'd tell 'em where I was. The little son of a bitch told 'em, and they still didn't believe him."

"Is he dead?"

"Pretty near."

That decided her. Without a second's further hesitation, she stepped in back of Slocum and untied the knots. While she worked, panting, Slocum told her how he had tried to get past the bodyguard, but was thrown out, and how two of the letters had dropped out of his pocket.

Once released, he saddled and bridled his horse as fast as he could. He did not know how much time he had left before they would be coming back from supper. He turned to thank her, but to his amazement she was busy saddling and bridling her own sorrel mare. Slocum thought it was for Octavio.

"Let the son of a bitch walk," he said coldly.

"That's between you and him," she said. "I'm riding with you, John."

Slocum stared. She was a beautiful woman, he thought. Her slender ankles were visible under the long coat. Her breasts filled the loose fabric of the coat.

"He's been sleeping with other women," she said. "Since I married him I've been faithful to him. Now it's time to make a fresh start."

Slocum did not want to travel with a woman. A pair like he and Mrs. Hunter would attract immediate attention. "But I don't know where I'm going," he said.

"You take the horses through the alley," she said, as if he had said nothing. I'll just get some warm clothes. I'll go out the front door; they won't notice that. I'll meet you on the other side of Washington Street. It's dark, nobody'll see." She walked out.

Slocum looked at Octavio. He led a horse out of a stall and hoisted Octavio onto its bare back. He'd be goddamned if he would saddle it. Like all the people from the Chimayo country, Octavio was a superb horseman. Slocum handed the boy a scrap of rawhide.

"Make a hackamore, Octavio," he said coldly. "And then go home and stay there. I don't ever wanna see you again, *entendido?*"

"*Sí,*" Octavio croaked. He fumbled with the rawhide. When he had made the hackamore, Slocum slipped it on the horse. Then he led the three horses along the alley. Once they were in the street Slocum looked up at Octavio, who was bent over the horse's neck, whimpering in pain. Slocum thought that the boy looked awful.

"If they find you," he said "they'll hang you in a second for a horse thief. So get up to the Chimayo country as fast as you can, then let the horse go. Or you can walk from now if you want; it's all the same to me."

"No, no!" Octavio gasped through his broken teeth.

"*Adios,*" Slocum said. He watched the horse move to the north. Well out of earshot, Octavio kicked his spurs into the horse's belly.

The front door opened. A figure in pants stood in the lighted doorway. Slocum grew taut, but as soon as the figure moved toward him in the dark, he recognized Mrs. Hunter.

They mounted in silence and moved off immediately. She was wearing her husband's clothes. The pants were a bit tight, Slocum noticed, and her breasts strained against the cotton fabric of the blue shirt. In her right hand she carried a pillowcase.

They trotted quickly to the east. Slocum had decided to retrieve the letters, give them to her, and let her burn them. As they rode beside each other she reached into the pillowcase and showed him a big hunk of baked ham and a loaf of bread.

He grinned. Then she took out a .45 and handed it to him. Next she pulled out a box of cartridges. "They keep them in a drawer under the rifle rack," she said. "I picked everything up on the way out. They were too busy drinking to notice."

Slocum smiled more broadly; this woman would carry her own weight. He shoved the cartridges into his saddlebag and looked at her with approval while she tied the pillowcase to her saddlehorn.

"All right, then," Slocum said. He jammed his spurs into his horse's flanks.

"Why so fast?" she yelled as she caught up with him.

"As soon as they realize we've gone, they'll think I went to pick up the letters. And they'll bet the letters'll be close to where they picked me up last time."

Slocum handed the letters to Molly. He tied the slicker to his cantle. When he had finished he turned to look at her. She sat her saddle as she held the package in her hands. He could not see her face in the darkness.

"Tear 'em up if you don't want to read 'em," Slocum said.

"No," she said finally. "My husband knows about them now. The harm is done. So there's only one thing to do. Keep 'em."

Slocum nodded.

"In case they catch up with us, we can do some horse trading," she said. "The newspaper is real hungry for 'em, not to mention Joe Gill. So let's keep 'em and play them for our ace in the hole."

He turned. Not even the man's jacket she was wearing could thin down the look of her lush body.

She said, "What do we do now?"

"Where do you want to go? I'll see that you get there."

She shrugged. "No place. Where are you heading?"

"Mexico."

"Mexico! All the way down there?"

"Sure. Your husband's the governor of this Territory?"

"Sure. What about it?"

"Governors're friends of other governors. He'll wire them to keep a lookout for me. So that leaves out Arizona and Oklahoma, and Texas, and Colorado, and Kansas. Leaves me Mexico."

"It sure does," she said with a rueful smile.

"But we got some advantages. It'll be warmer. I can get work on one of those big haciendas. The Terrazas spread is always looking for hands with trailing experience. And we can live off the land pretty good on the way, plenty venison."

"John, I'll ride with you."

"What'll you do when we get there?"

"I'm like a cat. I always land on my feet. Maybe start a high-class whorehouse. Save up enough to retire on."

Slocum admired her. She had spoken without any self-pity.

"O.K.," he said finally. "We got some hard riding. They must know by now we've gone."

6

"How'd he get away?"

"Damned effen I know. I—"

Hunter slammed his fist on the kitchen table. Juanita, the cook, promptly turned and left. She had experienced the governor's fits of uncontrolled anger before.

McDermott put his elbows on the table and grinned. Hoffman had been cut off in the middle of a sentence. A faint reddening of his cheekbones indicated his suppressed annoyance. McDermott was enjoying the big man's anger.

"I know, that greaser did it! You told me he was as weak as a day-old kitten, no need to concern myself with him!"

"I don' unnerstan' it, Gov'nor, I coulda sworn—"

"Incompetent fools! That's all I'm surrounded by, god damn it!"

"Yeah, we'll git 'em both," Hoffman said.

"What're you waiting for?"

"Gosh, no point runnin' after 'em in the dark. Can't see tracks, can't see no one to talk to who mighta seen 'em ride by—"

"And they took my wife's horse! I paid twelve hundred for that goddamn mare, my God! When you get 'em I'll hang 'em for horse stealing!"

Juanita padded in. *"Señor,"* she began. He waved her away.

She stubbornly remained.

"Juanita, later!"

"Señor," she said, "the *señora* ees gone."

"What?"

She beckoned him to follow. Hunter went upstairs. Her nightgown was thrown carelessly across her bed. Her underclothes, boots, and some treasured trinkets were missing. He stormed downstairs.

"Jesus Christ!" he yelled. "They kidnapped her! Pete, you know where the telegraph operator lives?"

"Yeah, out on the Cerillos road."

"Wake him up and tell him to get to the telegraph office right this minute!"

Hoffman asked, "You wan' us to ride after 'em now or wait till daybreak?"

"If you wait, no chance of catching 'em at all. If you take off now, you got a chance. Which direction you plan to take?"

Hoffman rubbed his chin and thought. "Hell, if I was them, I'd head fer rough country. The kind o' country where people ain't friendly to the law."

"Chimayo?"

"Yeah. Chimayo."

"Go ahead. I'll telegraph every sheriff in the Territory to round up a posse and watch out for them. If you get them, don't kill them. I want to ask some questions. You got that straight?"

"Yeah," Hoffman mumbled. He shot a vicious look sideways at McDermott. Someday soon, he decided, he'd have to teach that little bastard a lesson. He could shoot the son of a bitch in the back and claim they'd been drygulched by Slocum. No way to prove he was lying.

He brightened at the thought. McDermott left for the stable while he went to the kitchen and waited for Juanita to prepare sandwiches for the next day.

Danny found it hard to sleep. A noisy game was going on between Joe Gill and some drunken trail bosses. They had just delivered herds from Texas to some Colorado ranches, and were proceeding to the Pecos country in a leisurely manner. They had collected cash for their cattle. All of them had lost their wages to Gill.

Rendered careless by the free whiskey Gill kept setting in front of them, and grateful for the excellent cigars being handed to them, they were loud and exuberant. Gill had introduced a marked deck into the play. He was winning almost every hand, since the stakes were enormous by now.

The trail bosses had begun to gamble with their employers' money. The yelling and the slamming of the cards on the table were too much for Danny. He got up from his bed of old burlap bags and walked outside.

He took several breaths of the night air. It was

unusually warm. He decided to walk to the Plaza. The few Pueblo Indians who were still there were rolled up in their blankets.

Danny sat down in front of his favorite pillar. He had just settled down with a cigarette when McDermott cantered by on his errand. That was interesting. Danny's slow mind was still probing when McDermott trotted back twenty minutes later with Isaac Deakin, the telegraph operator. Deakin rode badly, with both hands grabbing the pommel of his spavined nag. He bounced all over the saddle.

This was getting more interesting, Danny thought. He put out his cigarette and walked to the end of the portal. By craning his neck in the shadows, he could see the two men dismounting thirty feet to the north.

Deakin was complaining about being awakened so rudely.

"Stop yer yappin'," McDermott said in a cold, toneless, bored voice. "Gov'nor's on the prod."

"What's up?"

"Miz Hunter been kidnapped."

"Oh, my. Oh, my!"

"Don't bother me!"

Danny tugged Gill's sleeve again.

"Beat it!"

"Mister Gill—"

"Beat it, Pop," one of the trail bosses said. "I feel I'm gettin' lucky. An' you're spoilin' my concentration."

Danny bent down and whispered loudly in Gill's ear.

Gill turned and stared. He took the cigar out of his mouth and stood up. He seized Danny's elbow.

"Yuh can't leave *now!*" one of the players said. "We gotta git even."

Gill paid no attention. "Listen," he said viciously to Danny. "You been drinkin'?"

"Hell, no," Danny said in an offended tone. He tried to pull his elbow from Gill's strong grip.

"Good," Gill said, satisfied. "Don't start now, you son of a bitch. Listen good. When that telegraph man finishes sendin' them emergency telegrams, he's gonna ride home. Know where he lives?"

"Yeah."

"You saddle up one of my horses. You be there waitin' for him when he comes home. Here's twenty bucks. Give it to him soon's he writes down the messages Hunter sent."

"S'pose he won't give 'em to me?"

Gill smiled. "Then tell him Joe Gill knows he won't want his house burned down sudden-like, an' if Joe Gill hears of anyone plannin' to do that, he'll try 'n' stop 'em. But he don't give any guarantees. Got that?"

"Hey, Gill! Come on back an' set down!"

"Don't make any mistakes, Danny," Gill said softly.

"Sure, Joe. You bet, Joe."

"Or we'll all be mighty sorry."

Gill watched Danny weave through the crowd. He turned to the two silent gunmen who acted as bodyguards and bouncers.

"It's slow tonight, boys," he said. "Better get some sleep. You're gonna have to do some hard ridin' in a couple of hours, my guess. Load up with plenty of cartridges. Pack some jerky an' a few quarts of oats."

He waved them away and sat down to the game. He was so absent-minded planning his next moves with Mrs. Hunter that he lost the pot. But he didn't care. The kidnapping was a startling development. He would have to plan his next moves very carefully.

Gill put the sheet of paper down on his desk.

The telegraph operator liked his house and didn't want anything to happen to it. So Hunter's telegrams had been repeated word for word.

Gill stared at the wall opposite the desk. It held nothing but a garish calendar issued free to cattlemen by Clay and Company, Commission Merchants.

The sun was still an hour below the horizon. Gill decided to let Dave Poole and Jim Blunt sleep as long as it was still dark. No sense riding off wildly in all directions.

There were, as Hunter had wired the governors, two men and a woman. Their trail, Gill decided, would not be too hard to follow.

The problem was, where would two men go who had the governor's wife as prisoner? They must have realized that her husband had the power to galvanize not only state and territorial forces into activity, he could also ask for federal marshals.

So where would the kidnappers head for?

There was only one answer: Mexico.

As soon as the sun rose above the Sangre de Cristos, Gill sent for Poole and Blunt.

Octavio was riding a very distinctive horse, a tall *grulla* gelding. Its grey color attracted attention immediately. He swore; he had the feeling that people would remember him because of the horse.

Octavio was right. When Hoffman began asking, as soon as he reached the Chimayo country, if anyone had seen two men and a woman riding together, and then described the horses, everyone said no, but told him a fine *grulla* with a lone rider had passed earlier.

So Hoffman and McDermott went after the *grulla*. Hoffman figured they might as well; they had nothing else to go on.

There was a hot springs two miles west of Terrero. By the time Octavio had reached it, he could barely hold on to the pommel. His body was one large bruise. All he wanted to do was to soak himself in the hot medicinal water until the bruises began to heal.

He finally reached the hot springs and dismounted with a moan of agony. He dropped the reins and stripped naked. He waded slowly into the hot water, groaning with pleasure as the waves of heat comforted his beaten body. Then he kneeled; as his body adjusted to the temperature, he sat down and groaned even more. He closed his eyes and dozed.

The sound of hooves startled him. He opened his eyes.

Two Anglos were looking down at him.

"Where's Mrs. Hunter?" the bigger one asked, almost kindly. Octavio shook his head in terrified ignorance.

The smaller man sat his buckskin with a forward crouch. He made the frightened Octavio think of a wolf on horseback. His cold eyes were alert and watchful, like the eyes of a wolf.

"Como está, amigo?" McDermott asked.

Octavio trembled.

"Donde está Señora Hunter?"

"No sé, no sé!" wailed Octavio.

McDermott dismounted. He walked back and forth, cutting for sign. He picked up the *grulla's* reins and walked back.

"Well?"

"No sign."

"Think the greaser knows?"

McDermott turned and stared with his cold wolf's eyes at Octavio, whose legs were trembling now, even though they were immersed in hot water.

"Nah. He's too scairt to lie."

Without any warning he jerked his Colt and shot. The bullet made a small hole as it entered Octavio's forehead, but it blew apart the back of his skull.

"You oughtn't'a done that," Hoffman said, calmly enough.

"Why not?" McDermott said as he reloaded. "I know someone who'll give us four hundred for that *grulla,* no questions asked. If we came back with the greaser, we'd have to bring the *grulla* with him."

Hoffman considered this. The body was floating on its back with a red cloud blossoming around its head. After a few seconds he said, "Yep. Who's this guy who'll buy it?"

"Up Rio Chama way. He'll blot the brand."

"O.K. We'll git rid of it there an' then say we went scoutin' thataway." They rode off without a backward look, the *grulla* trotting obediently behind them.

As they wearily rode through a narrow barranca that penetrated the northern slope of the Black Mountains, a bullet shattered against a rock wall. Bits of hot lead splattered against the flank of Slocum's horse. It whinnied and bucked. Slocum controlled the animal easily while he stared upward at the rock rim that loomed far overhead.

He saw nothing, but he did not expect to. The trail along the barranca was barred by huge boulders that had fallen from the high rims; other huge rocks had been washed down by cloudbursts. There was no way a rider could possibly make good time along that obstacle course. They were completely at the mercy of anyone up on the rim.

Molly Hunter started to spur her horse. Slocum reached out and grabbed its bridle. The horse plunged and danced sideways till it calmed down.

"What the hell's the matter with you?" she screamed. She reached out and tried to jerk the reins from his hand.

"We're getting a warning," Slocum said. "I want to know why."

He lifted his right arm palm outwards in the universal peace sign. He held that position for five seconds. Then he let the arm fall.

He placed both palms on his saddlehorn and waited.

Thankful Smith said, "Gol dang it." He did not curse when he was angry. He stood up on the rim of the barranca and yelled down, "Jus' hold it thar!"

A breeze came down the length of the barranca. It was hot, as if it had been radiated from a baker's oven.

"I want to get *out* of here," Molly said. Her voice was close to the breaking point. She was trying to control her fear.

"Stay," Slocum said calmly. His eyes searched everywhere.

As if on cue, thunder rumbled overhead. The horses trembled.

"Stay? *Stay?* What do you mean, 'stay'?" Why don't we run for it, damn you?" Her voice began to rise as she fought to keep control.

"If he wanted to kill us a little while ago, he could

have," Slocum said. "If he wants us to hold still a while, I'll accommodate him."

"Afraid?" she said with contempt.

"Yep," Slocum said pleasantly. "Besides, ma'am, I'm mighty curious who that man is. Indeed I am."

They waited.

Five minutes later a tall, thin man of sixty-five or so, Slocum judged, stepped into the barranca fifty feet ahead. It seemed to Slocum that he had materialized out of the solid rock.

He cradled an old single-shot Springfield in his left arm. He had a long, shaggy grey beard. His blue-grey eyes were sharp as tacks and missed nothing.

"Come a fur piece?" he asked placidly. His eyes were looking over the both of them, itemizing everything.

"Not too far," Slocum said. The old man had the look of a mountain man, he judged, a man who had simply let the wave of civilization flow past him.

"She come all the way?"

Slocum was not surprised that the old man had immediately figured his companion to be a woman. The handmade moccasins the man was wearing, the buckskin pants, the sharp, intense gaze—all these were typical of the mountain men. Their very lives depended on their noticing *everything*, no matter how seemingly inconsequential, and then making fast and accurate judgments.

"All the way, yes."

The old man grunted. He was pleased that Slocum had not tried to bluff and deny that his companion was a woman. He was silent for fully a minute. Then he suddenly asked, "What you folks ridin' here fur?"

"Headin' for Mexico."

"Most people want t' hang on to their scalps, friend, they go 'longside the river."

"So I hear."

The old man stroked his beard with a brown, strong, sinewy hand.

Molly suddenly prodded Slocum with a forefinger. "Let's go," she said sharply.

"Don' be in such a hurry, ma'am, we got things t' settle afore you goes anywhere." He turned to Slocum.

"Seems to me you're asking a lot of questions, no offense intended," Slocum said. Old men who lived in isolated places were very touchy, he knew.

The old man nodded calmly. "Yep. Tell yuh my reasons real soon. Young lady, ef yo're thinkin' to run that there Colt into my belly, take a look up top."

She tilted her head back. The top of the barranca was lined with Apache warriors.

Slocum knew when to yield.

"This is the governor's wife," he said. "We're being chased. Figured if we'd come this way, we'd stand a good chance of escaping them."

The old man grinned. "Kidnapped 'er, hey? She don' look kidnapped."

"I'm going with him of my own free will!" Molly snapped.

"Reckon yuh are," he said.

"Then we'd like to continue on," she said sharply.

"Can't say I blames yuh, ma'am," he said regretfully. "But yuh can't ride more'n a couple hunnerd yards without my say-so. Better calm down while I figger what t' do." He thought for a few seconds. Then he added, "Better come on up. Got a place up on the rim. You c'n rest a while while I send out messages."

"Messages about what?" she exploded. "We don't have time for games!"

Slocum said softly in her ear, "Shut up, god damn it." He turned to the old man and said, "Lead the way."

They walked and led their horses. The old man moved as lithely as an athlete one-third his age. When he reached the rim of the barranca he was not even breathing hard.

The Apaches stared at them silently. Their faces were painted for war, with black, jagged streaks running across their cheeks.

"Lucky it was rainin' las' night," the old man said. "Their bowstrings were wet. They didn't offer t' fight. Now they're rarin' t' go. Only reason they let you two by today was becuz I felt like talkin' English. Gettin' mighty rusty, only talkin' 'pache. Thar's my cabin."

A small cabin made from pine logs was set snugly in a hollow. It could not be seen until the viewer was almost on top of it. A narrow little creek ran past it and continued along on its way under clumps of pine. Slocum knew that the cabin location had been shrewdly chosen for its concealment value. The old man silently pointed to several rainbow trout that were holding their position in the current.

"Ain't many houses whar the food comes right t' the door," he said.

The old man said he had cut the logs and notched them. He had built a stone chimney with seven different channels for the smoke to dissipate. "Spreads the smoke around so much that unfriendly people don' notice it. Come on in an' set. I don' get no visitors 'cept 'paches. They ain't much fer gossip. Don' hev no newspapers along, hey?"

Slocum shook his head. He was beginning to like the old codger. One of the Apaches, a stocky, heavily muscled man in his thirties, suddenly spoke in an angry tone.

The old man listened politely. The other Apaches pressed close. They glared at Slocum and his companion, still not realizing that the other white was a woman. She paled and moved closer to Slocum. One of the Apaches noticed the movement and laughed. Slocum knew enough of the guttural Apache tongue to realize that the warriors wanted to kill both of them and get back to hunting deer.

The word "Belighanna" was repeated again and again. It was the way Apaches pronounced "American." Each time it was pronounced the Apache's hand moved unconsciously toward his knife hilt.

Finally the voices ground down to a halt. The old man stood up. Looking intently at each face, he spoke briefly and without any show of emotion. One of the Apaches started to interrupt. He stopped abruptly. He had just realized that he had violated the basic law of Indians in council: *never interrupt*.

The old man finished. He moved his arm, bent at the elbow, in a swift horizontal gesture. The discussion was over. The Apaches stood irresolutely for a moment in a sullen group. Then they slowly withdrew.

The old man watched them leave. Then he turned to Slocum with a grin. "Eat first," he said. "Then we powwow."

• • •

"I live pretty good up here," the old man said. He gnawed at a broiled venison rib. "Betcha thought I'm some kinda Injun chief, them takin' orders an' all. Fust of all, m' name's Thankful Smith. Nope, my folks warn't religious. Got married over in Sonora, married too young. Married a Mex gal named Linda. She got plumb disagreeable. I worked our li'l ranch like a mule, but she was allus complainin'. So one day I says, 'Linda, we ain't gettin' along.' She spoke pretty good English, she was pickin' up my way of talkin'.

"'Dang tootin',' she says.

"'Perhaps we better split,' I says. So she says, 'Half of everythin's mine an' don' you fergit it,' she says, nasty-like.

"'That's the way it's gonna be,' I says, real nice.

"So I took a saw an' cut ever' goddamn hunk o' furniture in half. Bed, chairs, sofy, chest. She was yellin' somethin' dreadful, but I kept on sawin'. Then I come to the mirror what 'er mother guv 'er when we got hitched. Cain't saw a mirror, yuh say? Absolutely right. I broke it all up in li'l pieces with a hammer. Then I got a scale an' weighed it. I dumped her half in a bucket. An' I walked out. An' I ain't seen hide nor hair o' Linda Smith pretty near forty years now, an' that's how come I took the name Thankful.

"So I come up here, green's green could be. Hired out to a Frenchy outa St. Louis an' larned trappin'. Lived with Mandans 'n' Blackfeet 'n' Utes. Got three, four Injun wives, any one of 'em better'n Linda. Dropped a colt here 'n' there. One day I come into these mountains lookin' fer beaver. It was pretty well trapped out up in the Rockies.

"I din't know these here was sacred mountains to the 'paches. They b'lieve the Thunder Gods live here. That's coz there's beaucoup thunderstorms bangin' 'round here most of the time. Storms drop water, water—everythin' needs water. So when I come up here a bunch o' 'paches out huntin' deer grabs me when I'm sleepin'. They was gonna see how fur they could go afore I starts yellin'. But jus' afore they puts me in the fire, head first, they start goin' through my saddlebags. In one of 'em I had a sponge. I picked it up somewhar, an' it was all scrunched down 'n' flat.

"It looked awful useless ef yuh din't know what it was fer. So it got tossed aside. I saw it fall in a puddle o' rainwater. I started makin' passes over it with my hands, like I was a magician in a tent show. They sort o' looked at me like I was crazy, then they saw the sponge. It was swellin' up. They backed off. I made more passes at it an' it swole some more.

"So they decided I was plumb full o' medicine, they din't know good or bad, an' they sure wasn't takin' no chances. Jus' as my hair caught fire, they pulled me out. They started treatin' me real nice, jus' in case I mought be bringin' sickness or somethin' terrible, like sendin' the deer away. Warn't easy t' learn the lingo. Took me ten, eleven years. I talk it real good now. I jus' tol' 'em you wasn't prospectin', jus' passin' through. Y'see, there's gold here, veins right on the surface. Once the miners come in, that's the end o' the huntin' 'n' all. Yuh *are* passin' through?"

"You bet," Slocum told him.

"Good. Yuh better git some sleep. You 'n' the lady

look plumb tuckered out. Your hosses are gettin' a good feed in the *vega* beyont the cabin. I'm gonna send word along the range to leave you people alone. What happens arterwards ain't none o' my business. This cabin's a bit tight fer three, so I'll be sleepin' with them. I got an ol' flour sack fer a towel ef the lady wants it, an' I got some of that Injun soap they make outa *sotol*, in that can thar. See yuh in the mornin'."

"I'm mighty grateful."

Thankful Smith shrugged. "Gotta practice American afore I fergit it. G'night."

7

An old grey-bearded farmer named Patricio de la Torre rested on his shovel. He had been repairing an irrigation ditch; the ditch was filled with trash and choked with weeds.

"No, *señores,*" he said. "I seen nobody. Jus' people what live in San Miguel, thassall."

"You stay here all day?" Hoffman demanded curtly.

"*Sí.* Sunrise to sunset."

"An' you ain't seen nobody?"

"Christ almighty!" McDermott exploded. "Ain't he jus' said so? Let's go!"

They trotted off. Hoffman was thinking hard. He suddenly reined in, cocked his right leg over the horn, and rolled a cigarette.

"Shit," McDermott began. "I—"

Hoffman lifted a commanding hand. McDermott

subsided. He turned and looked at de la Torre. The old man was leaning on his shovel as he stared at the two riders.

"What the hell you lookin' at?" McDermott demanded.

"Shut up," Hoffman said quietly. He smoked and thought. The heat in the airless valley was broiling. McDermott was restless. He took off his sombrero and fanned himself. "What the hell we waitin' for?" he asked.

"I'm thinkin'," Hoffman said coldly. "Somethin' you never git 'round to."

"Yeah?"

"Yeah." He took a long drag on his cigarette and threw it away. "Let's go south," he said decisively.

"South? Why the hell south?"

"Because they ain't come this way. They sure ain't been east, no strange riders been that way. West is Jicarilla 'paches 'n' Utes, too risky. That leaves south."

He turned his horse.

"Well, I ain't so sure," McDermott began.

Hoffman rode on without saying a word.

After a few seconds McDermott, angry because Hoffman had not bothered to respond, followed. He began cursing monotonously.

"Shut up," Hoffman said, without turning around.

"When we git 'em," McDermott said, "they're gonna be sorry-lookin' people."

"What you talkin' 'bout?"

"When I git finished with 'em they won't even be good fer dog food. You'll see what I mean. Jus' you wait."

* * *

Danny said, "I jus' seen Hoffman 'n' McDermott."

"When'd you see 'em?" asked Joe Gill. He yawned and laced his fingers behind his head.

"On San Francisco Street. They was loadin' up with bacon, beans, 'n' stuff outta the side door o' the Governor's Palace. Packin' it in their saddlebags. Shoved in 'bout five boxes of ca'tridges that Hunter brung out for them. When they got loaded they headed south like they was in a hurry."

"What they look like?"

"Aw, come on, Joe, y'know what they look like!"

"No, dummy, I mean, was they dirty, like they'd been ridin' a long time? Needed a shave bad?"

Danny pondered. Finally he said, "Yeah. That's the way they looked."

Gill thought. Hoffman and McDermott had been riding hard, for days perhaps. Given the situation, they could only be on the trail of Molly Hunter.

He made his decision. "Saddle Old Nick," he said as he turned to go upstairs and change into rough clothing. "Tell Dave Poole and Jim to get ready. They're ridin' with me."

Danny did not move.

"What the hell's the matter?" Gill said. He peeled off his coat and waited.

"They're sleepin'," Danny said.

"Wake 'em up!"

"They don' like it much when I wake 'em."

"Jesus Christ! Wake 'em!"

Hoffman reined in. The sombre mass of the Black Mountains loomed ahead of them.

"Bet they're in there," he said. Black jagged peaks

filled the horizon. Very little was known about the range.

"Not me," McDermott said. He scratched the week-old stubble of his beard.

"Why not?" Clouds boiled over one of the peaks. They could see the brilliant white flashes of lightning striking the peak but they were too far east to hear the thunder.

"Why not? Why not? B'cause," McDermott said, as if he were explaining something to a child, "it's full o' 'paches."

"Tell yuh sump'n," Hoffman said, turning his heavy shoulders so that he faced McDermott. "That's jus' what a smart hombre would think. An' he'd know some idjit like you would be thinkin' the same thing. An' he'd come to the conclusion that no person in his right mind would walk off into them mountains."

"What'd I tell yuh?"

"Yeah. So I figger that'd be the way he'd go."

"But—" McDermott stopped. He was puzzled. He couldn't figure out where Hoffman was going with his logic.

"A man's gotta think six, seven jumps ahead," Hoffman said, turning back once more to study the mountains. "You an' me, we got guns. No 'paches gonna jump us if we keep our eyes open all the time. I bet a double eagle we find 'em in there. Wanna bet?"

"Bet!"

They rode for the dark range while purple thunder clouds boiled around the crests.

Joe Gill, Dave Poole, and Jim Blunt rode hard. At Socorro, below Albuquerque, they were only twenty miles behind. Their horses were fresh compared to those of Hunter's men, and they had made excellent time. Poole and Blunt resented being sent on this search, but they were smart enough to keep quiet about it. Gill paid well, and he was a hard man to disagree with.

"Look at that," Dave Poole remarked. He pointed downwards. Horses' hooves had flung lumps of dirt backwards. "Movin' fast, wasn't they? They're on to sump'n, that's for sure."

"Yep," Gill said. "Let's slow down a bit."

"What the hell fer?" demanded Blunt. He wanted to get all this over with. Gill had a new girl working for him named Martha, and Blunt wanted to get back to her for some passionate screwing.

"Because," Gill said, "I wanna let 'em do all the work. An' when they've gone an' done it, you two are gonna mosey on up an' take what they got. Like pickin' real ripe peaches. I'm turnin' back. You two handle it."

Two oak logs glowed in the fireplace. The outside air was chilly; Slocum and Molly Hunter had bathed in the creek with the soap Thankful Smith had provided. It was after midnight. They had eaten well. Slocum was exhausted. He lay on his stomach, his arms and legs outthrust as he slept.

Molly, sleeping a few feet away, awoke to a faint rumble of thunder. After that it was hard for her to fall asleep again. She turned her head. In the firelight she saw the livid scars that crisscrossed Slocum's back. She reached out and delicately touched a wide, eight-inch-long scar that stretched across his lower back, the result of a saber slash made by a Union cavalryman at Chickamauga.

He awoke with such speed that she was startled. He gripped the hand that had touched him with a ferocious intensity that surprised her. When he realized that it was her finger that had touched him and not an enemy's hand, he released her.

She rubbed her wrist. "You're like some kind of an animal," she said tersely.

He stared at her. The firelight cast the deep cleft between her breasts into a deep shadow. His gaze drifted down to her man's shirt. The top two buttons were not fastened. She caught his stare and slowly began to unbutton the rest of the buttons.

Her tongue thrust into his mouth. It slid around and around his tongue, sucking and licking with all the skills she had learned in her long career.

He unbuttoned her pants and pulled them down. She stepped out of them. Her legs were long and slender. They gleamed white in the firelight. He turned her around and cupped her breasts from behind. She placed a hand on top of each of his, and pressed them against her nipples as hard as she could.

"Two," Nachodzil said. He sat down cross-legged across the fire from Thankful Smith. Smith was stitching a tear in his moccasins. It was near noon. Two strips of venison were broiling on a green stick.

Nachodzil was a scout who watched the eastern approaches of the Black Mountains.

Smith stitched in silence for a few seconds. "Guns?" he said finally.

"Each carried a horse gun," Nachodzil said. Apaches did not distinguish between carbines and rifles; indeed, they had no words for such distinctions.

"Pack mules?"

Nachodzil shook his head and stared with longing at the broiling venison. "Take one," Smith said, and continued to think.

Nachodzil snatched a stick from the coals and chewed the meat with enthusiasm.

Smith punched a hole in the leather with an old nail. It was far more efficient than his old bone awl. This business about the two whites without pack mules was significant. Prospectors always came with pack mules. The mules carried their flour, bacon, coffee, frying pan, drills, picks, dynamite, blasting caps, fuses, and so on. Prospectors were not mountain men; they did not know how to live off the country for their food.

So they were not looking for gold. They were traveling too light. And no one ever entered the Black Mountains. The mountains were not on the road to anywhere; they were not a short cut to anywhere.

"Did they seem experienced?"

Nachodzil nodded. "They looked everywhere when they rode. When they ate breakfast they made a very small fire. Very small."

So they knew what they were doing. Thankful did not like the sound of them at all.

"Mexicans, you think?"

"Americans. They kept looking for tracks."

So *that* was it. They were following the man and the woman who had come the day before.

"Shall we kill them?"

Thankful deliberated. "No. It will be too difficult. They are probably good shots. As long as they keep moving, do nothing. If they look as if they are going to stay, there will be plenty of time to kill them."

Nachodzil nodded. He rose and began to trot back

to his guard position eight miles to the east. It would take him about an hour. When he reached his favorite vantage point, a flat rock screened behind a grove of wind-shaped piñons, he sat down. The trail was far below. It quivered in the heat haze. Farther to the east the brown curving arc that was the Rio Grande flowed on its long trip to the Gulf of Mexico.

The two white men had stopped to take a siesta in the noon heat. They were almost directly underneath him. Unfortunately there were no boulders on the cliff edge for miles, or else Nachodzil would have pushed one or two over the edge and disobeyed Thankful's orders. Forty years before, two Americans had invited his tribe for a good party and free blankets and whiskey. When they sat down a concealed cannon loaded with rusty nails and scrap iron blew them apart. Two of Nachodzil's grandparents had died that day.

Thankful Smith's curiosity, which had always been of a large order, now impelled him to take a closer look at those interesting strangers. Especially since another scout named Juh had told him about the second pair.

Nachodzil, after all, was rather young. Perhaps his observations had been colored by boredom. The best thing, Thankful decided, was to go see for himself. The couple who were staying at his cabin looked as if they could use more time to rest. The woman seemed exhausted. If they were riding to Mexico, another day would be good for her. Besides, another day spent by their horses grazing on the nutritious grasses in the little valley would restore them in preparation for the hard stretches ahead.

Thankful set out. He walked in long, sinuous, ground-eating strides which covered distance surprisingly fast. Decades of living among Indians had given him the pigeon-toed walk which by now was second nature to him.

Hoffman leaned forward to pick up a blazing twig to light his cigarette. It was twilight. From the corner of his right eye he caught sight of something moving. To a less experienced eye it was simply the flash of the wings of a crow soaring from one branch to another among the far-off piñons.

But Hoffman was more observant. The supposed crow had moved from behind one rock to another. That in itself was not extraordinary. Still, crows usually moved from tree to tree rather than from rock to rock.

Hoffman continued to watch from the corner of his eye. The black patch suddenly moved once more. This time Hoffman was ready for it. It was the black hair of an Indian. He was using cover to come closer. Hoffman thought the man was very likely a scout. If that were so, the scout would then report to someone else, probably a leader of a war party. Things could become very complicated. If a war party should appear Hoffman might find it impossible to continue chasing Molly Hunter; it would be wiser to drop the whole thing rather than wind up spread-eagled between two trees while the war party worked him and McDermott over for an hour or so.

Most of the Apaches in the Territory spoke some Spanish. A little talk with that scout could prove useful. Pete McDermott was very good at that sort of thing. If Hoffman grabbed the scout McDermott could get the information out of him which would enable Hoffman to decide whether to press on or to drop the whole thing. The thought of McDermott torturing an expert at torture was so intriguing that Hoffman emitted a low chuckle.

"What yuh laughin' at?"

"Pete," Hoffman said, "when's yore birthday?"

McDermott was suspicious. "What you wanna know fer?"

"C'mon, Pete. What's the day?"

McDermott reluctantly said, "September fourteen."

That was three weeks away.

"Pete, how 'bout a birthday present?"

McDermott stared at him. "You drunk or sumpin'?"

Hoffman chuckled again. "Pete, you jus' wait. I'll take the first watch." ¬

"All right with me," McDermott said. He wrapped himself in his blanket, leaned back against his saddle, and was snoring in five minutes. When McDermott slept he slept hard, and he usually slept an unbroken eight hours. Nothing short of a rifle shot could wake him.

Hoffman waited till it was very dark. He was sure he was being observed by the Apache scout up on the slope. He let the fire go out entirely. Then he bunched up his blanket and slicker until they formed a dark mass. At a distance it could be considered a man asleep.

He stood up and began walking quietly along the trail toward the area where he had first seen the scout's head. For all his bulk, Hoffman could move as quietly as a stalking cougar.

He walked softly. The moon rose. Now he could see the rocks and worn trail in the canyon. He walked a quarter of a mile. He remained close against the cliff wall, which lay in shadow.

Anyone looking down from the slope could not see him. Sooner or later, he knew he would find an easy slope upwards that would take him up to the rim. In his favor was the knowledge that any scout sent to observe the two strangers would never consider that he would in turn be hunted by the men he was observing. And especially since the scout would be able to see the sleeping forms of the two men now that the moon was up.

Indeed, Nachodzil did exactly what Hoffman had estimated he might do. Moreover, Nachodzil, tired because of his long hike that day, had simply gone to sleep as he waited for sunrise to see what the two Belighanna were up to.

Nachodzil was on his back, asleep, with his two arms flung wide. Hoffman stood over the sleeping boy. The Apache was used to cold and did not need a blanket, although the nights were chilly. He wore a dirty red bandanna as a sweatband and to keep his shoulder-length hair out of his eyes. He wore a dirty white shirt and a breechclout which had once been white and was now a dirty grey. He wore a pair of moccasins with long uppers that could be pulled up to his knees for protection in thorny underbrush or cactus. Around his waist an old, worn leather belt held a beaded sheath.

Inside the sheath was an old Green River knife of the kind much favored by the old fur trappers. It was excellent for skinning beaver or deer. In a pinch it could be used against a grizzly when there was nothing else handy, and it was deadly against humans. It had belonged to Thankful Smith, who had given it to Nachodzil when he noticed that the boy only had a worn old butcher knife.

Thankful had used the knife for all those purposes. Now he was too old for fighting, but he was old enough for strategy.

Hoffman pulled out his Colt and erupted in laughter. The startled boy opened his eyes, but Hoffman had knelt down. The muzzle of the Colt was pressed into Nachodzil's left ear.

When Hoffman was sure that Nachodzil was awake he pulled back the hammer. Nachodzil froze at the metallic *click*.

Thankful padded silently through the darkness. The trail followed the natural contours of the land, a long, winding canyon. Thankful had gone up and down it so many times over the years that he could almost do it with his eyes closed. So now he moved without any sound except the soft padding of his moccasins.

The night hunters were out. Owls and rattlesnakes were searching for field mice. Once Thankful heard a soft *whoosh!* as an owl soared overhead with a squeaking mouse writhing in its talons. Thankful registered that as a normal night sound and paid it no further attention.

Night noises and movement were something he considered normal, much to the awe of the Apaches. They were afraid of the night, feeling sure that vengeful spirits of the dead were abroad in it, and the fact that Thankful went out in it without any sign of fear confirmed them in their belief that he was a powerful shaman.

Around a bend in the canyon he saw the shadows

cast on the rock wall by a fire. Thankful moved in absolute silence.

Nachodzil was lying on his back. His legs were tied at the ankles. A riata held his wrists together. McDermott was squatting next to the boy's head and shoulders. He had used Nachodzil's old knife, the gift from Thankful, to cut off the Apache's right index finger. By the time Thankful had arrived the blood had coagulated on the stump.

A rope sling supported Thankful's old Springfield. He unslung it, plucked a cartridge from one of the pockets in his deerskin jacket, and put the cartridge into the open breech. He closed the breech quietly and shoved the bolt forward. He had done this enough times, and he knew that his survival depended upon absolute silence.

A few feet in front of him a piece of driftwood stuck up where it had been left by a cloudburst earlier that spring. It would make a good rest. He estimated the distance to the campfire at about ninety feet. He stepped over a rock on his way to the driftwood log. A diamondback rattlesnake was coiled there. When the foot came down beside it, it struck.

The snake was six feet long. A blow delivered by a muscular snake of that size felt as if Thankful was being punched in his right thigh by a strong man. Thankful could not control himself. He let out a muffled cry of astonishment. McDermott's hearing was excellent. He shoved Hoffman hard and kicked out the fire as Thankful fired.

The bullet screeched along the canyon as the Springfield boomed in the confined space. It missed and shattered against the canyon wall.

The snake's fangs had gone through the buckskin

pants Thankful was wearing. It was a big diamond-back, and its poison sacs were full. Thankful knew he had to start cutting fast.

Hoffman whispered, "Move along left, I'll take the right." The two men began their approach, using the shadow of the canyon walls to mask their approach. Any other time Thankful could have handled the both of them. But in all his life on the frontier he had never been bitten by a diamondback, and that was the thing he dreaded most.

He inserted another cartridge and fired at a shadow. He missed because of his haste to get away and work on the snake bite. It was a fatal error. Hoffman and McDermott immediately fired at the muzzle flash. McDermott's bullet carried away the bridge of Thankful's nose and his left eye.

Thankful inserted another cartridge and fired at McDermott's flash. The loss of his left eye spoiled his depth perception. He missed again. The bullet raked a gash along McDermott's right cheek.

He cursed and ran a dirty palm across it. Someone would have to pay for that.

It was time, Thankful decided, to get out. He turned and tried to run. In spite of his age, he could run fast, but his venom-inflamed leg would not bear his weight. He stumbled and fell. By the time he struggled to his knees the two men were on top of him.

One of them twisted the Springfield from his grasp and smashed the butt across his face. Thankful groaned and went down.

"Christ," McDermott said ten minutes later, "I thought first the bugger was an Apache. Then I seen his beard."

"He's a goddamn renegade," Hoffman said. "You

better stop wipin' that face with those dirty hands. It's gonna get all infected."

"It's gonna leave a scar," McDermott said angrily. He turned and kicked Thankful in the ribs as hard as he could. Thankful grunted and lay still a moment. He had been talking to Nachodzil in Apache.

"Listen to 'em jabber," Hoffman said. "Throw 'nother log on the fire. I wanna get a good look at the ol' son of a bitch."

McDermott dropped a small driftwood branch on the fire. Blood was dripping from his cheek and splattering onto the shoulder of his dirty shirt. Hoffman stared at Thankful's leg. It had swollen a good deal in the last five minutes. Two small holes in the buckskin with yellow fluid oozing out of them told the story.

"Well, looka that!" he said. "The ol' bastard's snakebit!"

McDermott wiped his hand across his cheek and looked at the bloody palm. "He's gonna have a lot more on his mind real soon," he said with a tight smile. He picked up Nachodzil's knife and tested the blade on his thumb.

"Real sharp," he said with a grin. He turned toward Thankful.

Two hours later Thankful finally told McDermott where Slocum and Molly Hunter were. The agony caused by McDermott's skill with the knife and the effects of the snake venom were too much.

Nachodzil had died under the knife an hour before, but he did not say anything. The purpose of his death was to demonstrate to Thankful what would happen to him if he did not talk.

Thankful's leg was twice its normal size now and rapidly turning black. McDermott was sweating. A scab had formed over the cut left by Thankful's bullet. The pain had stopped, however, and he was smiling with pleasure as he looked down at his work. Hoffman did not like McDermott to drag it out as long as he did, but McDermott enjoyed it very much and Hoffman had to admit that the Texan was good at it. He always got them to talk before they died. He had failed with the tall stranger in Hunter's stable, but he probably would have succeeded if they hadn't broken off in order to eat. No question about it, McDermott was a valuable aide, and had to be humored along.

Satisfied, McDermott stood up and stretched.

"Hey, Pete," Hoffman said, "looks like you're finally gonna ketch up with that son of a bitch." He threw the saddle blanket over his horse, smoothed out the wrinkles, and dropped the saddle on top.

McDermott said absent-mindedly, "Yeah. Guess so."

Hoffman turned. McDermott was standing over the dead Apache. Not much had been left of the boy's face.

"This goddamn Injun," said McDermott with a disgusted tone. "Why, he don' have no necklace." His tone implied that Nachodzil was guilty of a bad lapse of manners. Hoffman was accustomed by now to McDermott's habit of looting dead bodies. A post trader would give fifteen or twenty dollars for a good silver and turquoise necklace that an Apache might have traded from the Navajo.

"Take the Springfield," Hoffman said wearily. "It's worth a few bucks."

"It's too damn old," McDermott complained.

"Yeah," Hoffman said, "but some Injun'll trade you mebbe a couple beaver furs. Ain't gonna hurt."

McDermott threw his filthy, sweat-soaked blanket over the back of his horse. Its back was covered with saddle sores.

"Yeah, all right," he grumbled. He threw the saddle on without straightening out the wrinkles in the blanket.

"Straighten out them wrinkles," Hoffman said.

"I'll git me 'nother hoss," McDermott said. "Hosses all over." He lashed the Springfield to the cantle.

"Don' look good fer the governor's guard to be ridin' a stolen hoss," Hoffman said in an irritated tone.

"Jus' don' worry 'bout it, Grandpa," McDermott said.

Hoffman looked at him. If he hadn't needed the vicious son of a bitch so many times in the past, and would probably be needing him again in the future, he would have gladly emptied a double-barreled charge of buckshot right into that sneering face. He sighed and turned away and mounted.

"What about the ol' bugger?" McDermott shouted. Hoffman had been thinking about their next move, and the fact that Thankful was still alive had escaped him.

McDermott usually liked to give the *coup de grace* by cutting the prisoners' throats. The old man's lungs were whistling as they tried to pump air while the poison gradually blocked the nervous system and rendered breathing more and more difficult.

"Shit," McDermott said conversationally, "he's shore a mess, ain't he? So what I'm gonna do, I'm gonna let you live, ol' man. How's that, ol' man?"

Thankful's one eye glared at them as his starved

lungs fought for air. "Effen it hadn't been fer that goddam rattler, both o' you scum would be belly up right now!"

"No use," McDermott grinned. "You got mebbe a couple hours more to live. An' it's gonna git worse. I wantcha to think 'bout that, ol' man."

He cinched the saddle and mounted.

"Yuh ketch up with Slocum," Thankful said, "an' you're gonna run into trouble."

"I'm lettin' yuh live a while longer," McDermott said, flushing with anger, "so shut yore goddamn trap!"

He did not like being told that there were men around who were tougher than he was.

"Pipsqueak! He'll be down on yuh like the hull Missouri on a sandbar!"

McDermott had heard enough. He ripped the Springfield from the cantle, reached into his saddlebag for the handful of Springfield cartridges he had taken from Thankful's pocket, and after loading it, fired.

Hoffman stared at Thankful. The bullet had entered Thankful's good eye and blown apart the whole back of his skull.

"Good shootin', huh?" McDermott said, as he re-tied the Springfield.

"Let's see what Slocum says," Hoffman said.

8

Juh heard McDermott's shot. The distinctive dull boom of the Springfield was unmistakable. By the time he reached Nachodzil's usual scouting position, from where he watched strangers as they entered the canyon, he had noticed Hoffman and McDermott as they passed deeper into the range. At first he thought that they were fleeing from Thankful's Springfield, and he smiled with pleasure at the thought that the two whites would unwittingly commit themselves into many more Apache hands.

Moving warily from rock to rock, taking advantage of whatever cover there was, he approached the two still figures lying face upward, and knew he was wrong.

When he had memorized every detail of what had been done to them he stood up, watching his back trail. He did not want to meet the two men who had done these things, especially since he possessed no firearms.

Clearly, they were hard men who would take pleasure in torturing him. It was important for him now to alert the entire Black Range about the two Belighanna. Burying the two dead men under a pile of rocks to keep off the scavengers could wait; this was more important. He trotted up to the rim top and began to run cross-country to save a mile and a half. Much to his surprise, he began to sob when he thought of Thankful. He did not think he could ever feel that way about a Belighanna.

"I want to say goodbye to the ol' codger," Slocum said. "But when I ask no one knows when he'll be back. Or they won't tell me. They don' trust me. It's time we left."

He went out into the meadow to catch their hobbled horses. Molly had washed their dirty clothes and they had dried quickly, spread out flat on the meadow grass. A young Apache covered with sweat ran by. It was Juh. Slocum knew something was very wrong by the man's desperate intensity and the look full of hatred that he directed at Slocum. He ran to the *jacal* where he and the others slept.

Several men came out immediately. Without wasting any time, they began to run in the direction Juh had come from.

"Something's going on," Molly said.

Slocum stopped one of the Apaches. He asked in Spanish what was happening. The Apache angrily shoved off Slocum's hand.

Slocum patiently repeated the question in Apache. So few whites spoke their difficult language that the astonished man came to a halt and told him what was lying on the canyon trail.

Molly walked up and asked what they were discussing. Slocum did not like the news. He told her what had happened.

"Well, I'm sorry the old man is dead, but why're you taking on so? You act like he was a relative or something."

Slocum did not answer. He watched the scouts as, armed with bows and arrows and an occasional lance, they trotted toward the east. Some turned to look at the two whites as they went by. Their black eyes glittered with hate. Molly shivered. Slocum watched them until they disappeared beyond a grove of pines.

"I asked you a question!" she snapped.

"Sorry, what about?" He turned toward her.

"Never mind that just now. When are we leaving? I don't like the feeling we're the only whites within a hundred miles of here."

"Not sure we will now."

"What?"

"Look here, Mrs. Hunter! Listen carefully. That old man was our guarantee that we were gonna get through these mountains. Get that straight. He sends word ahead, no one stops us. You understand that?"

She looked at him, surprised by his harsh, angry tone.

"Well, god damn it?" he asked.

She nodded.

"Good. Now, how far d'you think we'd get before we'd be ambushed?"

"We've got good horses!"

"True. Yet, horses gotta rest, horses gotta eat. That's two places where they'd wait."

"But how are they gonna tell them ahead that we're coming?" She smiled triumphantly. "Especially when we'll go thirty miles when they can only run maybe fifteen at the most? Tell me that!"

"Look over your shoulder," Slocum said with a grim smile.

She turned. Four columns of dense black smoke were rising vertically in the still air.

"Signals?"

"Indian telegraph. Now listen to me good. I found out plenty. Two whites killed Thankful and the Apache boy. After they killed the two, they turned around and went back the way they'd come. When I asked what they looked like, Juh told me that one was heavy and one was light. They—"

"How could he tell if he didn't see them?"

Slocum said patiently, "By their tracks. They did not have a pack mule along, so they were not here to prospect gold. They took Thankful's rifle with them."

She paled.

"Anyone you know?" Slocum asked. She nodded. "Sounds like Hoffman and McDermott," he said. She nodded again.

"The bastards killed our only guarantee for safe passage," Slocum said. "Another reason to make 'em pay for it. For some reason—maybe they think there's too many Apaches—they think if they move farther inside here it's gonna be too dangerous. But they're not gonna give up on us. So I got to figure out what they're planning next."

Either he and Molly could continue on their way south and hope they'd escape ambush, or he could force the issue to a definite conclusion by trailing Hoffman and McDermott—something they would never expect. It would be very risky for Slocum. How could he take Molly with him? But leaving her behind with angry, resentful Apaches would be far more risky for her. She would have to travel with him. There was no other solution.

"Saddle up," he said tersely. When she asked where they were going he said, "Not Mexico. Not yet!"

As they rode the Apaches folded their arms and stared. They were like gunpowder waiting for a spark to set them off. It would not take much. Slocum did not even make eye contact, lest one of them take offense and explode. None of them made a gesture of farewell. He braced his back, expecting an arrow to slam into it any second. It took all his will-power to refrain from digging in his spurs, lying flat on his horse's back, and galloping out of there. But all he heard was the humming of the wind through the piñon branches.

Dave Poole reined in. Jim Blunt, riding beside him, rode on a few feet and then stopped.

"What's up?" Blunt asked. He stood in his stirrups for a better view.

"Two riders," Poole said briefly. He had better eyesight than Blunt. He pulled his Winchester halfway from his saddle holster, then said, "Aw, shit," and shoved it in again. If the strange riders would have seen the gun come out they would have taken offense. Poole did not want offense, he wanted cheerfully volunteered information.

The two figures had suddenly emerged from the valley toward which Gill's men had been riding.

After a while Poole said suddenly, "Hell, it ain't them."

"What was you gonna do, kill 'em?" Blunt, slow and lethargic, jerked his head at Poole's carbine.

"Naw. Gettin' ready, suppose them two buggers cut loose at us. This is wild country, Jim. I ain't kiddin', neither."

The two figures continued to ride steadily toward them.

"Know 'em?" Poole asked.

"Know 'em? How the hell am I gonna know 'em? I ain't never been this far south. This ain't my stompin' ground, Dave. They look like a couple tired cowboys jus' wantin' a li'l powwow. Look at them beat-up clothes an' all. Nice-lookin' hosses, though."

"Yeah. Peaceful lookin'." But he kept his hands on his pommel close enough to his holster, in case he had to get his Colt out quickly.

"See Hoffman 'n' McDermott's tracks? Goin' right into that valley where they're comin' out of. Mebbe they seen them sons of bitches. We'll have our powwow, all right. We got enough coffee left?"

"Yeah, enough."

"All right. Let's give 'em the peace sign."

Slocum watched the two men come to a halt and raise their right arms, palms outward. Then they rode in a tight circle, the sign that they wanted to talk.

"Who are they?" she asked.

"Don't know," Slocum said. "Don't like their looks much. No reason for any rancher to send cowboys into these mountains. They don't look like prospectors. They're sure not Indians. When we talk, just grunt. Leave your mouth open a bit, like you're simple. No matter what's said, keep smiling. I want 'em to get the idea real fast that any kind of talk with you ain't going anywhere. Better wipe some of that dust off your sleeve and rub it across your face. It's sweaty enough to mess it up. Ride with your shoulders hunched up. I don't want 'em to see you got tits."

"I'm not a fool!" she retorted. Her face was pale with apprehension.

"We'll argue later if you want," he said indifferently, his eyes on the riders. "Now start smiling."

They squatted around the small campfire.

"Much obliged for the coffee," Slocum said. He leaned forward and added softly, "My partner ain't quite right in the head, but he's obliged too."

Molly grinned and cradled the hot tin mug. Slocum saw with relief that her hands were very dirty. It helped to conceal the fact that her knuckles were not scarred or broken, a dead giveaway that she was not a working cowpuncher.

"What's it like in there?" Poole asked. Slocum thought that the man's tone was a bit too casual.

"All right, I guess. Plenty of grass. Not enough water, though."

"What outfit you two with?"

Slocum had seen by the men's hands that, although they might have worked as cowpunchers once, they certainly hadn't done so for a long time. He suddenly recognized Poole as one of the men who worked for Gill.

"Flying R," he said. He knew of the Flying R, which was located on the west side of the Black Range.

"Where's that?" Blunt asked. Slocum couldn't tell whether the question was meant to test him or whether Blunt was sincerely interested, the way an old-time cowhand would be.

"On the San Agustin Plains. Runs about five, six thousand head. Maybe forty, fifty miles that way."

Poole flicked a glance at the brands on their horses.

"Ain't ranch stock," Slocum said. He cursed behind his casual face; the horses were branded with Hunter's own brand. A knowledgeable cowpuncher would have memorized every single brand for a couple of hundred miles around, including additional details such as vent brands, trail brands, and earmarks. No sign of recognition dawned in Poole's eyes. Slocum thanked God under his breath that the men were saloon hangers-on.

"Good hosses," Poole said.

"Paid plenty for 'em, we did. Can outrun Indian ponies any time. Got to be able to do that 'round here."

Poole grunted.

"We got a couple hundred head missing," Slocum said. Molly nodded her head vigorously.

"We figured maybe they drifted 'round the northern end of the Blacks and come down this way. Looking fer water 'n' grass, maybe they went up that canyon back of us."

Molly's smile was real this time. She marvelled at the accomplished, relaxed manner in which Slocum was telling one lie after the other.

"Find any?" Poole asked.

"Hell, no. We rode in early this morning. Rode right out. Too much Injun sign."

"What about tracks?"

"We had a big rainstorm three, four days ago. Wiped out all tracks."

As soon as he said that he waited tensely for the remark that any experienced cowman would have made at this time. The remark would have been, "Rain don't wash out cow flop."

Poole said nothing. It was clear that his mind was on something else rather than this desultory talk about cattle that might have drifted off the home range.

It was time to ask some questions for a change. It was a normal thing to do. Slocum said casually, "You fellers riding for some outfit 'round here?"

Blunt looked at Poole. That single gesture of Blunt's told Slocum that the two men had something to conceal.

Poole sipped his coffee. He sensed the alert intelligence behind the question. He decided that simply saying "yes" would not be enough to satisfy this stranger. He believed these were men from a local outfit and any inaccurate response would freeze any more conversation. And he needed the information that this intelligent and knowledgeable stranger could supply.

"Nope," Poole said easily. "We were part of a posse lookin' fer a couple fellas up river quite a ways. The others dropped out north of Albuquerque. We figgered if we kept on we might ketch 'em."

"There ain't no reward out," Blunt said.

"In case I was thinking of getting in on some of it," Slocum said dryly.

"Well, yeah," Poole said. His respect for Slocum rose.

Nervousness made a muscle in Molly's right cheek twitch spasmodically. Slocum hoped Poole wouldn't notice it.

"Your partner don' talk much," Poole observed.

"Nope," Slocum said. "Hoss kicked 'im in the head when he was a kid. Don' hurt his ridin' none, though."

Poole kept staring at Molly. She responded with her empty smile. Slocum hoped she would not collapse under the strain.

"What's your name, kid?" Poole asked.

For a moment Slocum did not understand why Poole had said "kid." Then he realized it was because of Molly's smooth, unshaven cheeks. The three men all wore a two days' growth of beard.

"Name's Tom," Slocum said easily. "Hoss kicked 'im twice, kicked 'im in the throat. Broke his voice box."

Molly smiled at hearing the name of her character.

For some reason the mute cowpuncher fascinated Blunt. He dropped his voice and said quietly, "How is it ridin' with a dummy?"

Slocum put a puzzled expression on his face. He would have preferred to get away from this dangerous area of talk, but too fast a departure might have aroused suspicion.

"Hell, Tom's all right. He's plumb smart around cows, Tom is. And he don't keep talking to pass the time, the way too many waddies do."

That was enough idle conversation, Slocum judged. Blunt took the hint and flushed, but he dropped the subject. Poole seemed to have lost interest. Slocum made sure that he would not return to it with his next sentence.

"So you're interested in them two fellers we passed up the canyon." Slocum leaned over and refilled his coffee mug.

As Slocum had guessed, Poole and Blunt immediately dropped the subject of Tom. They looked at each other and grinned.

"You bet," Poole said. "What did they look like?"

"One of 'em was heavy. Dark hair, wide nose like someone once took a club to it. Big shoulders, weight maybe two hundred, two hundred ten. Rode a chestnut maybe fifteen hands."

"The other?"

"About five ten, weight a hundred sixty maybe, brown eyes set close together. Kind you wouldn't want riding back of you with a grudge."

"That's them!" Blunt said with a wide grin.

Poole said, "Tell yuh what they did, they burnt down a ranch house up near Los Alamitos, shot the rancher, man name of Grierson. Raped his wife and set fire to the house. They shot 'er too but she lived long enough to describe 'em."

"Dirty bastards," muttered Slocum, full of admiration for Poole's convincing lie.

"So thank yuh kindly," Poole said, with an air of satisfaction. "Oughta ketch up with 'em sometime t'night."

"Maybe not," Slocum said.

"We c'n handle 'em, don' worry," Poole said confidently.

"Got no doubt," Slocum said. "Question is, how you two gonna live in that canyon?"

"Don' getcha," Poole said, frowning.

"We seen what them two fellers did," Slocum went on.

Poole waited with a puzzled frown.

"They had a run-in with a 'pache and some old mountain man, all dressed in buckskin. Killed 'em. That tore it; 'paches gonna go on the warpath, for sure."

"Well?" Blunt asked nervously.

"Had any experience with Injuns?" Slocum asked idly.

"None t' speak of," Blunt said. He obviously did not like the idea of a run-in with hostile Apaches, Slocum noted. That made Slocum's idea much more possible.

"'None t' speak of'!" jeered Poole. "He means none, fer crissake. What you drivin' at?"

"Why," Slocum said, "they'll take it out on you, ain't that plain?"

"No, it *ain't* plain," Blunt said stubbornly.

"Why don' they take it out on the two what done it?" Poole demanded.

Molly kept her mouth open as she turned from each speaker to the next. Slocum thought she was doing very well in her role.

"Why," Slocum said patiently, "because they look like real hardcases to me. They're taking a big chance, moving on through the range. But don't forget, they got guns, and prob'ly the Apaches don't have none. They got bows and arrows, lances. Still, there's plenty Apaches up in the range. Plenty of deer for venison, berries, water. Real nice eating."

Blunt looked even more worried.

Slocum pressed on. "Lots of things 'bout Apaches a man better know if he wants to keep his hair."

"Yeah?" Poole asked. "What?"

"Well, to start with, they're real scared of the dark."

Blunt's eyebrows rose in skepticism.

Poole said, "Yeah. Now we know what they like eatin', 'n' all about the dark."

Slocum looked at him calmly, paying no attention to the sarcasm.

"Could be important," he said. "For instance, the night is filled with ghosts. Ghosts of their family, ghosts of people they killed. These ghosts want revenge. No way to fight ghosts. So, Apaches don't move at night. What that comes to is, the best way to travel in Apache country is at night, you see?"

"Makes sense," Blunt said.

"Lay up in the daytime. Move at night. When Apaches attack, their favorite time is just before sunup. People ain't up yet, they're sleeping, and that's the time Apaches ain't afraid, 'cause ghosts only move at night."

"Sure makes sense," Blunt muttered. He looked at Slocum with respect.

"You sure seem t' know a lot about 'em," Poole said. He looked thoughtful.

"Used to live with 'em."

"*Live* with 'em?"

"Yep." This was true. Slocum had once spent seven months with Chiricahua Apaches in the mountains south of Benson, over in Arizona.

"Savvy their lingo?" Poole went on.

"You bet."

Poole made his decision. "You help us get these two," he said, "I'll give you fifty bucks."

Fifty dollars was a month's pay for a cowpuncher.

"That ain't bad for two, maybe three days' work. You can always tell the ramrod you was lookin' fer strayed cattle, too."

"I'm not gonna risk my neck and Tom's neck in the Black Range for *fifty* bucks!" Slocum said indignantly. He was pleased with the way the conversation was going. He did not want to appear too eager to travel with Gill's men.

"Seventy-five," Poole said.

Slocum turned to survey Molly.

"Don't worry," he said as he turned back to Poole. "I guarantee Tom'll earn it. He can read Apache sign better'n me. And they'll be watching us soon's we ride into that canyon. We'll be seeing smoke signals real fast. Tom can read 'em real good."

"Guess we need 'em," Blunt said. Poole nodded.

"O.K.," he said. "We got a deal."

9

"Jesus," whispered Blunt.

They looked down at the mutilated bodies.

"How we know 'paches didn't do it?" demanded Poole.

Molly shook her head vigorously. She pointed to the boot tracks left by Hoffman and McDermott around the prostrate bodies.

Slocum said, "Tom wants you to look over the tracks. See where the boot heels dug in there where they dragged the Apache close to the fire? See where they squatted next to 'em?"

"Guess you're right," muttered Poole. His face was pale. Coyotes and vultures had been at the carcasses.

Molly hooked her thumbs in her belt while she considered the startling things Slocum was doing. First, he had convinced two of the men who were chasing him—and Hoffman and McDermott—that they needed *his* help. Second, with Poole and Blunt's help, he was going to track down the two who were chasing him. Thirdly, with Poole and Blunt forming a sort of an escort, he was going to move with her well-protected through hostile Apache territory. And, last of all, he might be able to maneuver both sets of pursuers into a position where they could wind up shooting at each other.

Poole had been bent over studying the tracks. Now he straightened up.

"See any Injun sign?" he demanded. Indian country made him nervous; he was not used to being away from a saloon.

Molly shook her head.

Poole looked at her. Slocum noticed that she had not been constantly searching the canyon rims, nor had she turned even once to scan their back trail. It was evident that Poole had observed this as well, and he made his remark before Slocum could quietly instruct her to get cracking in her new role.

"There ain't be any Injun sign 'round here," Slocum said easily. "Remember what I said? Any time there's been a death the ghosts hang around. There's *two* ghosts here. I doubt you'd find an Apache within two, three miles. Bad medicine carries that far. We move a couple miles more, then we watch for Apache sign. Ain't that right, Tom?"

Molly stared at Slocum, full of admiration for his quick thinking. She sensed the warning he had issued to her for her future vigilance, and the clever way in which he just delivered it. She nodded.

"You'll see," Slocum went on. "Tom'll start checking our back trail, the canyon rim, checking out moccasin tracks, signal smokes, coyote yells, things like that."

"Coyote yells?" asked Blunt. "Signal smokes?"

"Sure. Every goddamn Apache in the Black Range is gonna know we're here in about an hour. Coyote yells is how they talk to each other. How many we are, what direction we're heading."

"Shit," Blunt muttered.

"But we go the way I said," Slocum said cheerfully, "I bet we'll be all right."

"Yeah," Poole said, "you hope."

Luckily, just before sunset, Molly was the first one to see them. Four puffs of black smoke went up on the northern rim. A few seconds later, four more puffs followed.

She touched Slocum's arm and pointed.

"There they are," he said, and pointed them out to Poole.

Poole looked at Slocum with respect.

Blunt asked, "What they say?"

"'Four people coming.'"

"So they'll be waitin' fer us?" Poole asked.

"Always a possibility," Slocum said.

"Hell, more'n *possible*," Poole said. The tension in his voice was clear. Poole was a brave man, but the suspense of waiting for an Apache attack was not something he was looking forward to.

"What about the ones we're follerin'?" Blunt asked. "They signalled 'bout them too?"

Slocum looked at Molly as if he needed her expert opinion. She nodded.

"There's your answer."

Poole asked, "So they're waitin' fer *all* of us?"

"That's the way I figure," Slocum said. As the sun lowered, the temperature was rapidly cooling off.

"These fellers we're follerin'—they know enough to move at night?"

"Probably not," Slocum said. He was wary. He respected Poole's intelligence, and he did not know what the man had in mind.

"So if we move at night, what's to stop us from bumpin' into 'em in the dark? Then ev'ryone's gonna start shootin' at ev'ryone else. Hell, man, that's stupid. I don't aim to get gutshot accidental."

Gutshots were always fatal; there was no way to disinfect the wound.

"I wanna pick my shots too," Blunt said.

"Christ, yes," Poole said. "I don't want Jim shootin' me an' later on sayin' he's sorry."

"I ain't that lousy a shot," Blunt began indignantly.

Slocum held up his hand and sighed.

"Gentlemen," he said, "we ain't gonna bump into 'em in the dark. Tom an' me, we'll scout ahead. When it's clear, either one of us'll signal to you two."

"What's the signal gonna be?"

"We'll bark like coyote. Two short barks, then one long howl. Like this."

Slocum gave the signal.

Blunt laughed. Poole glared at him.

Juh sat cross-legged inside Thankful's cabin. When he judged the time was right, he stood up in a swift, practiced move.

The others fell silent. Juh, although he was younger than most of them, had a certain driving force of personality which had become more pronounced after

Thankful's death. It was as if Thankful being alive had been a blanket covering this trait; when he died, the blanket was removed, with immediate results.

"Nachodzil was a fool," he began, without preliminary. It was not an Apache custom to speak critically of the dead; their ghosts might resent it and take revenge. There followed a shocked silence.

"I mention this so that none of us will be as blind and stupid as he was."

Dzali muttered in resentment. He had been a close friend of Nachodzil.

Juh waited until everyone had subsided.

"He permitted himself to be attacked while he was a scout. Why was this? I can only think that he must have been asleep. Can anyone think of any other reason? If so, speak."

Juh waited.

No one said anything.

Juh continued, "How could any Belighanna come up to an Apache secretly while he was awake? Well?"

"Thankful could," someone said.

"Thankful, yes. But no one else. And yet someone came up on Nachodzil. His shame is mine, and yours. Is this not so?"

Again there was an embarrassed silence.

"Then he tied him up and brought him down to the canyon."

Juh was an experienced tracker and had reconstructed everything that had happened.

He waited. Then he added, "I will not rest till this Belighanna and the other one are caught." He turned and asked, "Where are they now?"

A short, stocky man with a bulldog jaw and several parallel scars on his upper chest stood. A grizzly had clawed him once, but he had knifed it and killed it. He wore the claws of the grizzly for a necklace. He was respected. His name was Tildelan, or Bear Killer.

"At the cottonwood grove," he said. This was eighteen miles up the canyon. "They were arguing. Once they almost fought."

"This is bad," Juh said. "I don't want either of them killed fighting each other. That pleasure belongs to us."

The others grunted approval.

The scarred man said, "Four more Belighanna just entered the canyon, coming from the east."

"Guns?"

"All have guns."

"Pack mules?"

"None."

Juh frowned. He did not like what was going on, the sudden invasion of the valley by all these Belighanna. He did not understand it.

"Who is the scout?"

"My cousin."

"Take his place."

This was an insult to the scarred man's clan. His face darkened.

"I don't know him," Juh said. "I know you. *Take his place.*"

Tildelan pondered a moment. Then he shrugged and asked, "Now?"

"Now."

They watched Tildelan set off at a jog trot.

Hoffman lay on his back under a cottonwood. A woodpecker suddenly drilled into the trunk high above.

McDermott jumped nervously at the quick *rat-tat-tat*. He was sitting with his back against the trunk with one leg drawn up, carefully cleaning Thankful's Springfield. He always carried a small bottle of gun oil in his saddlebag, together with a few rags. He lifted the barrel and sighted along it. "Ol' bugger cert'n'ly kept it clean," he said, yawning.

"Nice 'n' cool here," Hoffman said. "But, Jesus, it's hot out there."

The canyon reflected the heat from the red sandstone walls and from the boulders erratically strewn about the canyon floor. Heat waves shimmered and shook. High up a hawk rode the thermals. Their horses nibbled despondently at the young cottonwood leaves. Not a breath of air stirred. Sweat dripped from their chins.

McDermott did not respond. He began tapping the ground lightly in front of him with a cottonwood branch that had fallen from the tree above him.

"Y' don' think it's hot?" Hoffman asked, so bored by now that he was willing to start a conversation about anything.

McDermott said nothing. After a while he muttered, "Seen worse." He struck the ground with sudden vehemence.

Hoffman craned his neck around the tree and saw that McDermott was killing ants.

"Why'n't you behave like a growed-up person?" he asked. "'Stead of like a goddamn baby. Oughta be home suckin' your poor mammy's tit."

McDermott's head turned slowly. His eyelids lowered slightly over his cold eyes. He put down the branch and splayed out his fingers across his right knee. He stretched his fingers a few times. It was an unconscious limbering-up exercise he usually performed before he jerked his Colt.

"Say again?"

Hoffman knew he had gone too far. He sighed. "Nothin' personal, Pete," he said softly. "Nothin' personal."

McDermott picked up the branch and went on killing ants. He did this with great precision and much pleasure. Hoffman forced himself to avert his gaze. He was afraid if he saw McDermott kill any more ants he would lose control and say something to the crazy son of a bitch that would set him off like a match dropped into a keg of gunpowder.

McDermott idly lashed the branch at a nearby dust-covered pebble the size of a pea. As it rolled over it gave forth a flash of yellow. Intrigued, McDermott struck it again. It rolled over and dislodged the dust on the other side. Now it shone yellow all over.

He leaned forward and picked it up.

As soon as he felt the weight of it he knew.

"Christ," he muttered. He flicked it toward Hoffman. Hoffman picked it up. His mouth dropped open in amazement. McDermott began to laugh.

"Dick," he said, "listen. We come here lookin' fer Molly Hunter an' the guy what kidnapped 'er. We don' find 'em, what's Hunter gonna do?"

"Tear our asses off," Hoffman said.

"Yeah. An' we're out of a nice job. But s'pose I got a gold mine? Man, what the fuck do I care?"

Hoffman noted that McDermott had said "I", not "we." He smelled trouble ahead. He watched McDermott bite hard into the nugget. For a second he wished that it was iron pyrites and that McDermott would snap off a couple teeth, but the soft metal yielded to the impression of McDermott's brown, tobacco-stained incisors.

It was gold, all right.

McDermott grunted with pleasure. He made one more test. He took out his jackknife and cut deep into the nugget. He held it up triumphantly for Hoffman's inspection. The yellow gleam continued into the slit.

"Thought fer a second it mought be a spent bullet," McDermott said. "Lotsa people been kilt in this here canyon, I bet. But it's real! It ain't fool's gold neither."

Hoffman said, "Question is, where's it come from?"

Neither of them knew anything about gold mining, not to mention anything at all about gold deposits in the Black Range. The Apaches had been very careful to kill any prospector who had ventured into the range to try his luck. None had ever come out. Therefore, no information whatsoever existed.

No one had ever found any free gold such as the nugget that McDermott had just found, not to mention the incredible ore bodies of surpassing richness that lay farther up in the canyons. The nugget McDermott had picked up had been eroded out of an incredibly rich vein up the tributary canyon that began fifty feet to their left.

"Where's it from?" McDermott repeated Hoffman's question. "I guess mebbe up there," he said, pointing up the tributary canyon.

He leaped to his feet. The streambed that came down to join the major canyon was dry, as was the canyon where they were resting in the cottonwood shade. McDermott walked out of the shade of the cottonwood grove and right into the glare of the sun.

He entered the dry streambed and fell to his knees.

He began to pick up pebbles at random. Every one that seemed unusually heavy was placed under his jackknife blade and sliced open.

The first five he picked up all turned out to be nuggets.

There is no sensation in the world quite like picking up a gold nugget. The weight of it is absolutely stunning. Together with the weight comes the realization that he who holds it and has discovered it may be wealthy for the rest of his life.

McDermott squatted on his heels and let out a wild Rebel yell.

It reverberated against the canyon walls. Even Tildelan, up on the rim, about to lie flat after he had told Ikali he was replacing him, heard it.

Hoffman hastily pulled on his worn socks and boots. He followed McDermott out into the broiling sun. When he reached the streambed he began to copy McDermott. Within five minutes he himself found three nuggets. Each was the size of a pea or somewhat smaller.

He straightened up and began thinking. McDermott was on the other side of the streambed, happily crooning to himself as he scrabbled in the dust on his knees.

Since the water flow would have diminished somewhat by the time the water was flowing on a level stretch, as right here, gravity would have forced the water to drop the heavier nuggets farther up. The smaller nuggets would have been pushed along to stop just about where they were. So, the conclusion: go farther upstream.

He stood up and walked past McDermott.

"Where yuh goin'?" McDermott asked.

"Lookin' around," Hoffman said.

A hundred yards farther in was where the higher pitch of the canyon began. Just about here, Hoffman reasoned, was where the heavier nuggets would have been dropped by the slackening current. The rock walls came closer together. The heat that blasted out from the walls and from the rocky surface of the canyon floor made Hoffman feel as if he was inside a baker's oven.

At random he picked up a lump the size of a walnut. As soon as he felt the weight he knew it was pure twenty-four carat. He felt pleased that his guess was right. He did not have a jackknife. He took out his Colt, set the nugget on top of a flat rock, and smashed the butt onto the nugget. The soft metal took the cross-hatched design.

"Jesus," Hoffman whispered. He shoved the nugget into his pocket. He began to test every pebble he saw. He paid no attention to the sweat that dripped from his face. "Oh, Christ," he muttered every time he found another nugget. In five minutes he found nine nuggets, ranging in size from large beans to walnuts.

He had completely forgotten the heat, the governor's wife, Slocum, the Apaches, and even McDermott nearby. The only thing that mattered now was the possibility that every pebble in this tributary canyon was a nugget. The more nuggets he found, the closer he was coming to a wealth he had never before dreamed to be within his grasp.

He became sharply aware of McDermott's existence when a shadow fell across him. Hoffman resented the interruption, and the thought that McDermott might be finding nuggets as big as his made him angry and apprehensive.

McDermott stared at Hoffman's bulging pockets.
"Found some, hey?"

"Some," Hoffman said grudgingly.

"Big ones, hey?"

Hoffman shrugged. McDermott took off his sombrero and ran his sleeve across his dripping face. His forehead was white, the rest of his face tanned.

"Got 'ny objections if I sorta worked near? Seein' as how if it wasn't fer me you wouldn't'a found one single bitty piece?"

Although McDermott's tone was that of a man idly conversing, his cheeks were flushed with rage. He had a nervous habit of biting his lower lip when he was about to explode, and he was doing so now.

Hoffman nodded his assent. He decided that this was not the time to push things to a violent confrontation. McDermott was a faster draw and a superb marksman. There were other ways to handle the crazy son of a bitch.

Hoffman suddenly realized that if he came back to Santa Fe without McDermott, nobody would give a damn. And if he came back with his saddlebags full of nuggets he could tell Hunter to shove his job. Hell, Hoffman thought to himself with a kind of exquisite delight, there was a lot more nuggets scattered along the canyon floor, no doubt about it!

And when he'd picked them all up, there'd be placer gold. He could find water somewhere up on the rim, and run it down below for washing out the gold dust. And when that would be all picked up, there *had* to be a rich vein higher up! Hell, he would become a rich man, richer than Hunter. He could buy his own ranch and stock it with fine breeding stock.

Christ almighty, his dream went on, some day *he* would run for governor of the Territory!

He began to chuckle.

McDermott said, "You goin' nuts?"

"Thought of a joke," Hoffman said with a wide smile. "Tell yuh some time." Under his breath he added, "If you're still alive, yuh rotten li'l son of a bitch."

Because Hoffman had suddenly realized that if Pete were dead, he could dump McDermott's saddle and use his horse to pack the nuggets out—the ones they'd already found, and the ones he was sure to find.

The next thing to do would be to make sure where the mother lode was lying. Then make a rock cairn, write out a claim, and—Christ, he didn't have any paper or pencil!—and then register the claim in the nearest county seat.

He looked up. McDermott had crawled ahead of him. The greedy bastard wanted to get ahead of him. McDermott's pockets were bulging with the nuggets he had already found. For a second Hoffman felt the wild, unreasoning anger that was typical of McDermott. He realized that if he were to kill McDermott, the man's gold would become his.

So what it amounted to was that McDermott was working for Hoffman. Without knowing it. For free!

He began to smile again.

"Hey, look at this un, fatty!" McDermott said, holding up a nugget in back of him without turning around. This nugget was the biggest one either of them had found.

Hoffman did not like being called "fatty," but this time he did not care.

When McDermott did not get a response he turned around. He triumphantly held the nugget aloft. Hoffman's smile became a wide grin.

"That must be some joke," McDermott said. "Lemme hear it."

"I'll tell yuh later, Pete," Hoffman said, beginning to laugh. "It's a great joke. Even you might like it. No kiddin'!"

10

Tildelan lay flat on his belly. He peered down three hundred feet into the canyon below. He asked himself in amazement, "What are the crazy Belighanna doing?"

Then he sighed. He wished Thankful was there; Thankful knew all about the crazy ways of the Belighanna.

Once more Tildelan looked down. The Belighanna were still crawling on their hands and knees. The fools seemed to be picking up stones and putting them in their pockets with signs of much excitement. They were not medicine stones: that is, they had not been struck by lightning, nor did they have shapes like those of animals, and hence might have been used for hunting charms. It was all a great mystery.

Finally he gave up. He slid back from the rim and trotted back to describe what he had seen to Juh. Juh had known Thankful better than all of them. Maybe

Thankful had told him something which would be of help.

"They are putting stones in their pockets!"

Juh nodded without any show of surprise. This calmness comforted Tildelan; he had confidence in Juh's judgment. Juh went back with Tildelan. The two of them lay flat and watched.

After a few minutes Juh noticed something very interesting. After he had watched the Belighanna for five minutes, he had observed that not once did they turn around to look at their back trail; not once had their gaze traveled upward to look at the canyon rim. *Not once.* This was not how knowledgeable people survived in the Black Range. What had saved their lives many times, Juh decided, was that they carried guns; any attack would have been too costly.

Still, even then, any frontiersman, guns or not, would have reconnoitered at least twice in that five minutes.

Juh looked at the cottonwood grove. The Belighannas' horses were tied to cottonwood branches and were contentedly munching the young leaves.

The men were up two hundred feet into the tributary canyon. They could not see their horses. Even if they were to turn around, they still could not see them.

Juh looked back at the Belighanna with contempt. Whatever they were doing, the horses should have been placed within sight. If they had wanted to leave their horses in the shade of the cottonwood trees, one of the men should have stayed behind to watch.

Without horses, the Belighanna died in this country. Either they were caught by Apaches, or the heat killed them. In those boots they couldn't walk. If they pulled the boots off, their feet would be cut to ribbons in an hour. A wise man never risked losing his horse.

Juh sat up, content. He stood up in full view of the Belighanna should they turn around and look up at the rim. Tildelan motioned for him to lie flat. Juh shook his head with a smile.

"What are you going to do?" Tildelan asked, shading his eyes from the sun as he looked up at Juh.

"Watch," said Juh.

He walked to the old deer trail that zigzagged down the canyon wall. Ages ago a crack had appeared in the canyon rim because of an earthquake, and a rough slope was the natural result. Over the thousands and thousands of years that had elapsed deer and bear had seen the green of the cottonwoods below and knew that there was water there. Paws and hooves had finally shaped the trail; when the Apaches came, they were quick to utilize it for the same reason.

He began to walk down. The trail was rough, and stones and pebbles of all sizes littered the steep angle of descent. A man who was careless could easily stumble and fall to his death. Juh moved with confidence. He had so much contempt for the two Belighanna who were scrabbling in the ground like medicine women searching for valuable herbs that he was sure they wouldn't even look up once. And suppose they did see him? A revolver bullet couldn't carry that far with any accuracy.

But this action would make for some excited retelling by Tildelan. That was one of the reasons why Juh had decided to come upon them so openly. Tildelan's word was taken as gospel by anyone who knew him, and Juh's status would correspondingly rise.

When Juh reached the canyon floor he walked calmly straight to the horses, with no attempt at concealment. He unhitched them. They had eaten till their bellies were distended, and made no objections when he took their reins and walked out. They followed him quietly.

Juh's heart leaped in triumph. He suddenly realized that not only were the Winchester carbines still in their saddle scabbards, but it was also probable that boxes of cartridges were in the saddlebags. These Belighanna were traveling light, and there was every reason to believe that they carried plenty of ammunition if they deliberately entered Apache territory. He stopped and unbuckled one saddlebag. His heart leaped. There were six boxes. He quickly checked the saddlebags on the other horse, which nuzzled him in a friendly manner while he was unbuckling the cracked leather strap. Eight more!

This made him rich. Carbine ammunition was very hard for an Apache to buy; the price was prohibitive, and very few whites—outside of the Comancheros who occasionally came up from Mexico—would take the risk involved.

Tied to the cantle of the fat man's saddle was Thankful's Springfield. This rifle had good medicine attached to it. And there was even more good news. The Belighanna had emptied Thankful's ammunition pouch made out of deerskin and the big cartridges filled the bottom of the other saddlebag.

Juh buckled the saddlebag. He felt exultant. This find—of two carbines, their ammunition, and the Springfield—had made him the most powerful Apache up on the rim. Not to mention the horses!

He led the horses up the deer trail. If the Belighanna were to turn around they would see him right away. They could run out of the tributary canyon, stand at the bottom of the trail, and shoot him. He had the carbines, true, but he knew he was a bad shot and needed much practice before he could hit anything.

But this was a risk he had deliberately chosen. He could have continued down the canyon a few hundred yards, mounted one of the horses, and ridden out that way. At the end, where the canyon broadened out into a valley, he could have then swung around and climbed safely back into the range without any risk whatsoever.

But risk was what he was seeking. With Tildelan for a witness to the danger he was deliberately courting by climbing up the deer trail in such an exposed position, he was displaying his bravery and contempt for the Belighanna. This style was more of a Comanche attribute than an Apache one, but it would certainly get him talked about.

This was very important for Juh. He was having trouble trying to impose his will on the strongly individualistic Apache.

So this feat, stealing their horses and their guns from under the owners' noses, would raise his status immeasurably. The next time that he would propose anything, from a brief trip behind the ridge to roast mescal to a war party against the ranchers in the Plains of San Agustin, people would think twice before making any objection. Had he not proved he had very good medicine?

He finally reached the rim. Tildelan stood up. His eyes were round in amazement and respectful admiration.

"You can ride this one," Juh said in a bored tone, although his heart was pounding with excitement. His entire calm demeanour would be recounted to the others, of that Juh was certain. He handed over the reins of McDermott's small chestnut. It was a happy accident that he had replaced the unreliable Ikali with the universally respected Tildelan.

Before he mounted Juh took one last look at the Belighanna far below. They were still on their knees. Suddenly Juh knew what they were up to. Thankful had once told him that Belighannas became like mad dogs as soon as they saw certain stones of heavy yellow metal. And when one Belighanna found the yellow metal, others followed, like the old buffalo stampedes. And like the buffalo they destroyed everything in their path.

It was time to let everyone in the Black Range know what was happening.

Eight miles to the east, Molly held up her right hand.

The three men following stopped.

She pointed to a faraway mountaintop. Three puffs of black smoke were rising in the still air. There was a five-second pause. Then three more went up.

"What's that mean?" Poole demanded.

Slocum, his eyes riveted on the smoke, said tersely, "Wait."

They watched. There was no more smoke.

"Well?" Poole demanded.

"They're announcing a council," Slocum said. "Right, Tom?"

Molly nodded vigorously.

"Council of what?" Blunt asked.

"They didn't tell us," Slocum said, poker-faced.

Blunt reddened.

Poole said, "Think it's somethin' t'do with us?"

"Them fellers we're following. Or us. No way of knowing."

Poole said, "What's your suggestion?"

"We either keep going, or we go back. I'm for going ahead."

Poole grinned. "Wanna earn yore seventy-five bucks, don't'cha?"

"You bet," Slocum said. "Besides, I'm mighty curious what's ahead."

"Me too," Blunt said. "An' I hear there's gold in thar."

"Jus' rumor, Jim," Poole said. "Jus' rumor."

When Hoffman discovered that the horses were gone from the tree where they had been tethered, he thought at first that they had broken loose, perhaps snapped off the branch by tugging for some juicy young leaves.

McDermott understood these matters better. "Yeah," he said, "Mebbe yours busted loose. Mebbe mine busted loose. But I'll be double goddamned if they *both* broke loose at the same time. Don't stand to reason, it don't."

"Well, I bet that's what happened," Hoffman said stubbornly. "They'll be close by. No reason for 'em to leave this fodder an' water to walk in that goddamn sun."

But they were nowhere to be found in the grove.

It was Hoffman who first saw Juh's moccasin tracks.

"Hey, Pete," he said. He pointed to them in silence.

"So what?" McDermott said.

"Whaddya mean, 'So what?'" Hoffman said angrily. "That's the end of the goddamn ponies. We got a long hike in front of us, that's what!"

"No, we ain't," McDermott said equably. He took out his Colt and checked the trigger action. "Don' cry, ol' man, I know how t' git our hosses back."

This "old man" style of McDermott's was new. Hoffman didn't like it, but he suppressed his natural instinct to retort.

"Yeah? How?" he asked shortly.

"We foller the tracks," McDermott said patiently. "At the end of the tracks is gonna be our hosses. Ain't that obvious?"

Hoffman disregarded the insulting tone and confined himself to thinking about what McDermott had just said.

Here was McDermott—who hated to walk—proposing that they trail an Apache on foot. And into Apache territory!

"Yeah, it's obvious," Hoffman said sarcastically. "An' effen I dropped a double eagle into a rattlesnake den on a warm evenin' jus' when the li'l darlins was about to leave home an' git their supper, it suttinly would be obvious all I had t' do would be to git on my knees an' stick my arm in the den. That shore is obvious. But I ain't gonna do it, not even fer a double eagle."

"Scairt?"

McDermott's contemptuous tone made Hoffman angry all over again. "Didja hear what I said?"

"Sound scairt t' me," McDermott said, with an arrogant smile. "I'll go git 'em myself, li'l boy." He turned and began to follow the tracks.

Hoffman stood for a moment indecisively. They could walk to Socorro, twenty miles to the northeast, and buy horses there. But that was a hard two-day hike, in boots. With their nuggets they could get anything they wanted, saddles, everything. But then word of a rich gold strike would spread through the town like a prairie fire fanned by a strong wind.

On the other hand, McDermott might come across the stolen horses by nightfall, if they had any luck. If there was a scout watching the horses Hoffman knew that the murderous little Texan would make short work with his knife, and with much pleasure.

What the hell, it might work.

"Wait a second!" he yelled. Just then the seams of McDermott's right-hand pocket burst open because of the weight of the nuggets. He stopped and cursed.

He picked them up. "I think we better cache the stuff," Hoffman said. "No way we can climb with that stuff weighin' us down."

"Yeah." He pointed. "You go round that end of the grove an' I'll go thisaway. We'll cache the stuff an' neither of us'll know where the other one put it. How's that?"

"O.K.," Hoffman said.

"Meet yuh here in ten minutes."

"O.K., Pete," Hoffman said. Sometimes McDermott's sensible ideas surprised him.

Up on the rim Tildelan watched everything. He shook his head in astonishment. Now the crazy Belighanna were hiding their completely ordinary pebbles under rocks. They were stupid. If an Apache wanted to hide something, he would never put it in the canyon. At any moment a thunderstorm, followed by a violent cloudburst, would send the rocks tumbling like children's toys, so powerful would be the rush of water.

When the two men had finished—it was clear to Tildelan they did not trust each other—they moved to the cliff edge. Obviously they were tracking their own horses. When they reached the place where the old deer trail began its long diagonal up the canyon wall, they looked up once as if judging the distance. Then they began the climb.

Tildelan slid back from the canyon rim and ran to tell Juh.

Slocum well understood the dangers of cloudbursts in the mountains. The problem was that the canyons were frequently the only way to enter the mountain ranges. Eternal vigilance was the price of safety, Slocum believed, particularly when, added to that problem, he faced unfriendly Apaches.

The solution was never to sleep in a canyon. If a man had to, then it had better be above the high-water mark. This was easy to determine. Lengths of driftwood and skeletons of squirrels, snakes, and coyotes which had been drowned in the sudden flood indicated high water.

Whenever he was riding in a canyon he always picked out places above high water as a refuge. There he would go, even if it meant he had to abandon his horse. He quietly mentioned this to Molly when they were riding a few hundred feet in front of Poole and Blunt.

"What about them?" she asked.

Slocum shrugged. "They're big boys," he said indifferently.

She accepted that. She asked, "What about the smoke signals?"

"There's only one way to find out," he said. "And that's to go up on the rim, find Juh, and ask."

"Suppose these two don't like the idea?"

He looked at her and said gently, "Ain't that just too bad, Molly?"

Slocum looked down at the tracks. He easily re-constructed what had happened. While Poole and Blunt let their horses munch at the cottonwood leaves, Slo-cum followed the tracks of each man. He saw where they had separated. One set of tracks led to the west end of the grove, the second set led to the east. Each set showed random wanderings, then finally stopped in front of boulders that approximated each other in size. Slocum guessed that each one weighed close to three hundred pounds. Each set of tracks showed that boot heels had dug into the yielding dirt as if the men were pushing something heavy with all their strength. Logically, the boulders had to be the objects that had been pushed. It seemed an idiotic way to pass the time in the broiling heat. Slocum dismounted and, with a grunt, pushed one boulder aside.

A slow smile spread across his face. He dumped the nuggets into a saddlebag. He left the boulder in its new position. He shoved aside the other boulder and then emptied those nuggets into the saddlebag. He left the boulder in its new position as well.

When the two men came back to claim their nug-gets, each would assume the other one had found his cache. As Slocum thought of indictment and coun-tercharge and angry denial, his smile spread further.

Then he turned and looked into the tributary can-yon. He was sure the nuggets had come from there. Some day, Slocum told himself, he would come back and check out that canyon. This little trip would bring in a lot more than seventy-five dollars, thanks to the pioneer work of Hoffman and McDermott.

So the damn fools, after caching their gold in this stupid fashion, had discovered next that the Apaches had stolen their horses in broad daylight.

It was a comedy, because the Apaches had probably watched every move made by the two fools.

"You're goin' *where?*"

"Up on the rim."

"What the hell fer?"

Slocum did not like the irascible tone employed by Poole. He was afraid that he might lose control as a result of it, so he forced himself to be very calm.

"Tracking 'em some more."

Poole and Blunt looked up at the rim. It was as tall as a ten-story building. Poole next turned and looked at Slocum.

"We seen what them buggers did to that ol' man 'n' that 'pache," Poole said slowly. His face showed revulsion.

Slocum waited patiently.

"Them 'paches, with them smoke signals they're makin', you say they want a council, stands t' reason there's gonna be a power of 'em up there."

"Stands to reason, yep."

"I c'n pretty well figger out what they'll do to any white man they ketch up there."

"You're probably right," Slocum said pleasantly.

"I want them two fellers," Poole went on. "But I don' want 'em *that* bad."

"I do."

Poole was not sure that he had heard right. "You *what?*"

"I said I do."

"Well, hell," Poole said. "I hired you an' I tell you I don' want you goin' up there! They ketch you an' it's gonna be like me shovin' my pecker into an anthill.

It's gonna hurt like hell even if I get it back."

"Well, now, Mr. Poole, I've got something to say."

Poole saw a red spot on each of Slocum's cheeks. Poole saw that this tall, rangy man had suddenly stopped looking like a dusty, tired cowhand. He now had the appearance of someone who it would be a good idea not to cross.

A little muscle pulsed at Slocum's jaw.

"What?" Poole asked.

"I'd be the last person in the world," Slocum said carefully, "to want to have something like that happen to you. But I'm going up there. And if you try to stop me, well, I don't like to talk about unpleasant things, but I gotta tell you I'll blow a hole in you big enough for a blind man to piss through."

Poole was a professional gunman and a good shot. He had heard enough. Besides, Blunt would have contempt for him unless he taught this shit-kicking cowboy a lesson.

He jerked his Colt. But the cowhand's right arm moved in a blur. By the time Poole's gun had cleared the holster, Slocum's gun was three inches into his stomach.

Poole was bent over, gasping for breath.

"You handle that thing like it's a siege gun," Slocum said.

"Son of a bitch," moaned Poole.

11

It was a hard climb up the steep trail in high-heeled boots. McDermott cursed steadily all the way up. He kept sliding back on the rocks that had been set at a sharp angle from the horizontal. Leather soles did not provide a firm grip, but since he only weighed a hundred and fifty pounds the going was not too hard for him.

Hoffman weighed two hundred and twenty and he was not in very good condition. The heat had destroyed the salt balance in his blood, and he felt weak. Somehow, sweating did not seem to affect McDermott. Hoffman was panting so hard that he had to open his mouth.

McDermott turned around. "Hey, Pop!" he called out, in a wickedly amused tone. "Need a hand?"

He turned back to face the trail. Hoffman stared at his back with intense, calm hatred.

"Nope," Hoffman said. Under his breath he added, "But you're gonna need a coffin."

He waited there, with his back against the canyon wall, until he caught his breath. It was several degrees cooler at this height, and the time—late afternoon—meant that the sun's blinding glare was no longer pouring down on them. He looked down at the tributary canyon far below. He could see the rock under which he had cached his store of nuggets. By turning his head and examining the rocks on the other side of the green expanse that was the cottonwood grove, he scanned several rocks—under any one of which, he knew, McDermott's gold cache might be.

It would be childishly easy to find it. All he would have to do would be to walk to each boulder in turn and pull it aside.

He decided that it was childish, really, the manner in which they had hidden their gold. They did it that way because it was easy; a little more hard thinking, and he could have found a far better hiding place.

"The heat musta fried my brains," he muttered.

"Shut up!" McDermott hissed viciously.

They were almost at the rim. The sun had gone down behind the high ridge to the west. It was twilight, and the air was cooling very rapidly. Hoffman waited, panting. McDermott, he noticed, was not even breathing hard. Hoffman thought that the little bastard was pretty good in his line of work. Indeed, they had done a lot of difficult things together. They had made a good team. With a start of surprise, Hoffman realized that he was, in a sense, composing an epitaph for the dead McDermott. But even good things had to end, so it was going to be: *Sorry, Pete*.

Hoffman saw a green flash at the edge of his vision.

He half-turned and drew automatically, as he went into a half-crouch, but with embarrassment he saw that it had only been a green lizard leaping straight up from a cactus. He was trying to catch a fat bumblebee colored a brilliant yellow. The lizard missed and fell to the ground.

McDermott whipped his head around, sensing Hoffman's draw. He was in time to see the fall of the lizard. He understood the reason for the excitement and gave a contemptuous laugh that made Hoffman feel hot all over. Many of McDermott's annoying little habits were things that Hoffman had judged over the years as not being important.

Now that Hoffman saw his way to financial independence—indeed, now that there was a strong possibility he would become a rich man—he was beginning to let his angry feelings well up.

It took willpower for him to let the hammer down easily on the Colt rather than point it at McDermott's face and pull the trigger. The only thing that deterred him was the fear that the explosion in this narrow canyon would be so loud that it would bring every Apache on the rim down on them in minutes.

Then he thought that there was an ironic kind of symbolism in the lizard's fall. McDermott had himself leaped for a golden prize. And if Hoffman had anything to do with it, McDermott, like the lizard, would take a fall.

Long ago the Apaches who lived on the rim had built a corral to hold the horses they had planned to steal from travelers and ranchers. The corral was a mile back from the rim, in a well-grassed and watered small valley.

But that was before Thankful's time. The old fur trapper had persuaded the Apaches not to kill the ranchers; reprisals would involve heavy army detachments with artillery. As for the travelers, all had decided that they should be permitted to go through the range as long as they made no attempt to settle in the mountains.

Prospectors were fair game. The trouble was that prospectors walked in. A man on foot sees the geology of the ground much better. They always had pack mules for their gear, but when the Apaches got up from the moaning ruin of what had been a man, all they had to put in the corral were mules. Later the mules were simply eaten. Apaches liked mule meat, which they considered far more tasty than beef.

The corral lay empty. It was not a good one anyway; the rails were so crooked that Thankful took one look at it when he saw it for the first time and said, "If we had a pig an' it crept through, it would never know whether it was inside or out."

Translated into Apache, the joke was meaningless. After one attempt to repeat it in council, Thankful dropped the phrase.

There was no one around when McDermott reached the corral. Before he reached it he told Hoffman to stay well hidden in the piñons, a hundred feet back of the corral. "I c'n git flat as a diamondback when I see an Apache, but yore ass sticks up like Mrs. Murphy's drawers, 'n' I c'n run faster too, case they decide to light out after me."

Hoffman recognized the accuracy of the remarks, although he didn't care for the way they were phrased. He was secretly pleased that the first contact with the enemy would be made by McDermott.

He turned on his heel without making any response. He found a sturdy piñon, sat down with his back against the trunk, and folded his arms. He hoped that son of a bitch would get himself scalped by a vigilant Apache scout. He would enjoy that; if it were to happen, he wouldn't mind the long walk back to Socorro. All he had to do was lie low till the excitement passed, make his way down the trail in the middle of the night, pick up all the nuggets, and start hiking.

He knew the station agent at Socorro, O'Connor, would give him a pass on the train up to Santa Fe; he wouldn't have to cash in any of the gold in Socorro.

At Santa Fe he could sell the gold without anyone having the faintest idea where it had come from. Then he could take it easy on McDermott's money—that was the way Hoffman worked it; he would be living on McDermott's money—until he figured out a way to go back to the Black Range and come back in one piece. With enough well-armed men, who were well-paid, it ought to be possible.

While he daydreamed he took off his boots. *Jesus Christ, no wonder!* The torn holes in his filthy socks had started blisters.

He began to massage his feet. He was completely unaware of the incongruous situation: massaging his blistered feet in the heart of an Apache stronghold while his partner was busily stealing back their horses from the man who had just stolen them.

Too many people were smoking in the cabin. Juh began to cough. Apaches had come in from all over the Black Range in response to his smoke signals. They had walked over to the corral and seen the two fine horses he had cleverly taken from the Beli-

ghannas. Tildelan had related his eyewitness account.
Since he was universally respected, no one expressed
any skepticism.

They had admired the two carbines and the boxes
of cartridges. Envy was obvious, which made everything all the sweeter.

Nevertheless, a man who possessed the kind of
good medicine Juh clearly did would find it easy to
get even jealous warriors to follow him. He intended
to propose a huge war party that would strike with
sudden savagery at the growing ranches that were
beginning to mushroom in the rolling plains below
the wild grandeur of the Black Range. After the raid,
he would tell them, they would come back with plenty
of horses, guns, and prisoners. Young boys could be
adopted into the tribe if they showed courage; the
young girls could be used for breeding and the older
ones for torture. It was a proposal that he was sure
they could not resist.

The two horses were standing near one another in the
center of the corral. They were still saddled, although
McDermott noticed immediately that the Winchesters
were gone from their saddle scabbards. So were their
saddlebags.

"Shit," he muttered. The reins were loosely looped
around the horns.

McDermott lay flat for ten minutes. Nothing moved.
A new moon rose in the east. With its help he still
saw no one.

He stood up, removed three railings, and put them
to one side. He walked to the horses through the knee-
high grass. They lifted their heads from their concen-

trated munching and recognized him. They had eaten their fill. They did not resist when he led them out. He replaced the rails.

"Let's go, fat boy," he said.

Juh decided to let the Apaches talk over the project. He was coughing from the smoke. He would give them half an hour, then he would start the formal council. There everyone had to be calm, serious, and dignified.

He stood up and buckled on an empty cartridge belt that he had won in a knuckle-bone game from a drunken Chiricahua. He opened a box of cartridges. Very much aware of envious stares, he shoved the cartridges one by one into the belt loops.

He picked up the Winchester. While everyone watched in envious silence, he ostentatiously worked the lever and jacked a cartridge into the chamber, as if he were used to this process.

Then he stepped outside. A full moon rode overhead. He felt lucky. Things were going perfectly for him. He smiled with satisfaction and set out for the corral. As soon as he noticed that the rails were down he knew something was wrong. First he thought that somehow the horses had knocked them down in their efforts to get out. He dismissed that theory: horses stayed in corrals. Besides, the rails would have had to be lifted out one by one.

The next idea that came to him was that a couple of the Apaches, stung by jealousy, might very well have stolen them and ridden them away. He bent over in a crouch. The grass only revealed that someone had stepped on it. It had happened only a few minutes ago; the grass was still rising. He had no way of knowing that it was boots and not moccasins that had crushed the grass.

Bent in a half-crouch, the furious Juh followed the tracks.

McDermott was waiting for him with his cocked Colt in his hand.

Juh suddenly sensed the figure standing in front of him.

He cried out, "Wait!" in Spanish. McDermott fired. Juh dropped the carbine and put both hands to his head. Only a trickle of blood oozed out from between his fingers as he died. McDermott bent down and unbuckled the gunbelt. He rolled the dead body over and pulled the gunbelt off. He buckled it on top of his own belt.

Hoffman puffed over and said, "Jesus Christ, we'll have the whole goddamn tribe on top of us!"

"How's *that*, fatty?" McDermott boasted, as if he had not heard what Hoffman had said. "Got our hosses back 'n' my Winchester too! Pretty damn good!"

Hoffman grabbed his horse's head and headed for the trail. He was in a fever to be off. He kept looking over his shoulder at the direction from which the Apache had come.

"They still got your Winchester, fatty!" yelled McDermott. "Wanna go back 'n' git it?" He fired a shot from his Winchester in wild exultation.

Hoffman thought that the son of a bitch acted as if he were drunk. He was absolutely sure that McDermott was crazy. "Y' wanna go back, I'll go with yuh. Say the word!" McDermott said.

"Let's jus' git the fuck outa here," Hoffman muttered. His heart was beating so hard he could actually feel it thumping. He had no experience fighting Indians and he didn't want to start.

Hoffman set a feverish pace as they slid and stumbled down the trail. McDermott followed, pulling Jug Head, his horse. He was laughing at Hoffman's frantic haste. Jug Head was nervous and kept balking.

"Come on, *come on!*" McDermott snapped. He had no patience with animals. His good humor disappeared. He jerked hard on the reins. Jug Head shied, slipped, and went over the side. There was a shrill neigh and then the men heard the sound of impact four seconds later.

"Now you've done it, you dumb little bastard!" Hoffman yelled, goaded beyond endurance.

McDermott said, with amazing calm, "Nobody calls me that. That goes fer you. We git down to the bottom. I'll let yuh pull first."

"Think yo're a better man than I am?"

"Soon's we git to the bottom," McDermott said slowly. His cold eyes had the look of a striking snake.

Hoffman felt a chill hand grip his heart, but it was too late to back down. He set one foot carefully in front of the other. He didn't want to wind up a heap of broken bones, like poor Jug Head.

Poole and Blunt had been impressed by one of the things Slocum had told them: *In Apache country, travel at night.*

This they proceeded to do.

It was after nine P.M. There had been a full moon earlier. Because of the fine visibility the two men had been tense, constantly watching the rim of the canyon, trying to peer into any area where the shadows seemed strongest. Blunt was more nervous. His mind produced Apaches behind every boulder. Twice he pulled his Colt and Poole said, "What the hell's the matter with you? You're jumpy as a virgin in a whorehouse!"

"Christ almighty," Blunt said, "I never been in 'pache country at night, that's why!"

The moon sank behind the western rim. Poole let out his breath.

Blunt started to talk, but Poole said angrily, "Shhh!"

Blunt tried to speak once more, but Poole whispered fiercely, "Shut up! You got 'ny idee how far sound travels up a narrer canyon? You wanna say sumpin, *whisper*."

Blunt subsided.

They moved on in silence. No sound came except the creaking of leather from their saddles and the occasional clink of an iron-shod hoof striking stone. Both men kept their hands on their gun butts. They were sweating with apprehension in spite of the cool night air.

McDermott knelt beside Jug Head. The horse's two rear legs were bent at sharp angles. Long slivers of bone protruded through the skin. He lifted his head and nuzzled McDermott. Hoffman thought bitterly that the horse had fallen because of the Texan's impetuous and careless behavior. Nothing good would come of it, he knew it.

McDermott made no sound of regret. He took out his jackknife and with an expert slash severed the horse's jugular. The horse quivered and his legs trembled. Hoffman did not expect McDermott to break into tears; after all, a horse was simply a means of transportation. Still, just about anyone else in that situation would have said something like "He was a good horse." The blood spurted in the air and some of it fell on McDermott's face. He wiped it away absent-mindedly, as if it had been a sprinkle from a sudden shower. Hoffman watched him with more revulsion than ever. McDermott searched through a saddlebag. It was empty.

"Help me turn 'im over, will yuh?"

"Ain't no way you 'n' me is gonna turn over Jug Head," Hoffman said. "He's a big un."

McDermott was angry. "Crissakes, I wanna see if some o' my ca'tridges is still in it!"

They had dropped their earlier quarrel. Hoffman had said it would be best to forget the whole thing, at least till they got out of the canyon. Their chances of survival would be better if they ran across Apaches, because two men could fight better than one. McDermott had grunted approval.

"Yeah, Pete," Hoffman said now. He wanted to placate McDermott. His earlier scheme of killing McDermott was postponed until they ran the Apache blockade. "But that son of a bitch weighs seventeen hundred pounds. An' I ain't et all day."

"Neither have I!" shouted McDermott. "Yuh think I been eatin' steak 'n' potatoes behind yer back?"

Hoffman's recent desire for peace flooded out of him. In its place the old anger flared up. He yelled, "You fuckin' insane li'l prick, I wouldn't put nothin' past yuh!"

In the darkness, on the far side of the cottonwood grove, Poole and Blunt heard the distant squabbling voices. They could not distinguish the language let alone the words. Neither one said so, but they proceeded on the automatic assumption that only Apaches would be so unconcerned about talking so loudly in Apache territory.

Poole whispered, "How many?"

Blunt listened. He had keen hearing. "I figure two, mebbe three," he whispered.

Poole was silent. "Yuh think we c'n get past 'em?" he said finally.

"Hell, no," Blunt whispered. "Canyon's too narrer."

Poole thought for a few seconds. "Know what?" he suddenly said. "They're yellin' so loud, they ain't worried 'bout nothin'. They prob'ly figger there's no one within fifty miles, mebbe."

"So?"

"So let's massacree 'em," he said simply. "I'm gettin' sick o' pussyfootin'."

Blunt began to smile.

"You bet," he said. They dismounted and dropped their horses' reins. The well-trained horses would remain there without moving. Very slowly the two men began to walk carefully through the cottonwood grove toward the voices.

When they were halfway through the grove McDermott saw that the ears of Hoffman's horse had swivelled suddenly. He knew that horses had very keen hearing. He had been about to try to lift Jug Head by gripping one of his front legs and hoisting it till the leverage thus gained would make the horse topple over on the other side.

Very slowly he let the leg down. He touched Hoffman on the shoulder and placed his finger to his lips. When Hoffman turned, McDermott pointed to the horse's ears and then to the grove. Hoffman understood immediately. He put his lips to McDermott's ear and said, "Bear? Coyote?"

McDermott whispered, "No. He'd take off. Probably 'paches crawlin' at us."

But by now Poole and Blunt were within fifteen feet. Hoffman and McDermott's squabbling had condemned them to death. Had they not been quarreling, McDermott would have noticed the horse's ears two minutes before.

They turned to face the grove. As they pulled their Colts Poole and Blunt suddenly saw the movement of the two figures in the darkness.

They fired just before Hoffman and McDermott saw them. In fifteen seconds each man fired his six shots at the center of the human figures opposite him. Hoffman and Blunt died immediately. Poole was shot in the throat and he lived half a minute. McDermott was mortally wounded—Poole's shot had sliced off the top of his heart—but he was still determined enough to knock out the empty loads and insert six cartridges. He smiled with satisfaction and lifted his Colt to fire at the still moaning Poole. Then he died, convinced, as were all the others, that they had shot at Apaches.

Slocum and Molly circled behind the cabin. They gave it plenty of room. They heard the sound of singing as the Apaches within proclaimed their war victories. Sticks beaten together provided a rhythmic counterpoint to the drumming sounds coming from stretched deerhide over an empty gourd.

Circling past the corral, Slocum was the first one to see the prostrate figure lying on his back in the tall grass. Juh had been blown backward by the impact of the heavy slug. The lead had gone through his front teeth and taken off the back of his head.

"Christ," Slocum said. He knew then that Molly and he had better get out of the Black Range as quickly as possible before someone found the body. Even though Slocum had been friends with Thankful, all that would go by the board. The revenge exacted on any white people would be vicious.

But the chances were that Juh wouldn't be found till morning; Slocum had come across him by accident. In the tall grass the body couldn't be seen until someone was practically on top of him.

It would be best to get out of the range and into the desert.

Well-fed and well-watered horses could outpace any Apache on foot, and the Apaches had no horses. An Apache could run seventy-five miles a day, but they couldn't outpace a horse across the desert if the horse had plenty of water.

Slocum let the horses graze to their heart's content on the nourishing grass on the rim. It was far better for them than the cottonwood buds and leaves they might find in the canyon.

In spite of Molly's nervousness at being up there with the drumming going on in the dark, Slocum forced her to be still while the horses munched away.

When their bellies were distended, Slocum, who had noticed that the nearby deer trail had signs of human use, decided to take it down to the canyon, and thence go out the canyon till he came to the desert. He would make it with an all-night ride.

They led the horses down the steep slope with care. They let the horses find their footing without rushing them; that was the safest way with horses on mountain trails.

As the light increased the horses moved faster, with increased confidence.

Molly was the first to see Hoffman and Mc-Dermott. She said with a strangled gasp, "There. There, *look*."

"My, my," Slocum said. He searched the grove and found the bodies of Poole and Blunt. He looked at them with a wide grin.

She had turned away. The horseflies had covered the blood with a mass of green and gold bodies; the buzzing of the gorged flies nauseated her.

Slocum felt a rush of joy. His plan had worked.

"Aren't you going to bury them?" she asked, her face pale.

He looked at her with a hard face. "If they had killed me, d'you think they would've buried *me?*"

She was silent.

"Well?"

"I guess not," she finally said.

She watched Slocum collect the guns. "Why do we need all those guns?"

"We don't. I don't want 'paches to get 'em." He tossed them into a tangle of fallen and rotting trees and branches. Next, he pulled off the saddles and saddle blankets of the three horses. Then he took Hoffman's *riata*, cut it in three parts, and then tied the bits of two of the horses to the bridle of the horse in front.

"Let's go," he said.

"Where?"

"Mexico."

"Why Mexico? All those men are *dead!*"

Slocum looked at her and sighed. He shook his head. "Your husband and Joe Gill don't know that.

D'you think they'll call off the whole thing when each of 'em finds out these hombres're dead? Those goddamn letters are worth too much. They'll find other men. I want to be over the border."

"I disagree."

"Well, god damn it, you want to ride alone through 'pache country? Good luck. Pick any horse you want and go." He turned his back on her and added, "Goodbye."

She set her jaw stubbornly. Then she yielded.

Slocum said, "All right. Now listen. With these horses we'll change every hour. Old Comanche trick. We'll always be riding a fresh horse, see? Anyone follows us, they gotta stick on the same one. After a couple hours' fast riding, carrying a man who weighs a hundred and eighty, hundred and ninety pounds, any horse gets awful tired. But we'll always be on a fresh horse. Now, before we waste any more time blabbing away about your great experience in Indian country, or how people ain't gonna want to kill us any more because a couple men just got killed, I'd like to put plenty of distance between us and here, if you got no objections."

She flushed and said nothing. She mounted her horse.

Slocum bowed and said, "After you, ma'am."

She flushed once more and set off.

Chie found the resinous shoots he was looking for. They were about the diameter and firmness of cornstalks. They were straight and tall. The leaves were blade-shaped.

A scout had come in and reported that two of the Belighanna were moving farther up the canyon. He

lit two stalks. Each flared up instantly and left a pe-
culiar little puff of black smoke. The range would be
on the lookout for any more Belighanna.

By common consensus the cabin belonged to Juh.
Since his spirit would cling to it, it would have to be
burned with all his possessions.

Since he had been killed by the two men who had
circled around the cabin during the night, they would
have to be caught and punished in a way Juh's spirit
would approve.

Chie was not an experienced tracker. He had made
a snap judgment based upon a superficial examination
of the tracks he had found around the corral.

The tracks were difficult to understand, especially
those made in the resilient grass. He had no idea that
two men had climbed up the trail and killed Juh, then
had gone down again with the two horses that had
been stolen from them.

There was a fierce debate which concerned whether
Juh's recently acquired carbine and Springfield should
be burned. Chie said that Juh's spirit would be satisfied if it could have the more desirable carbine. It
would not object too much, he felt, if the old Springfield happened to disappear from the cabin just before
it was to be burned.

Since there was no medicine man up there, or anyone old and wise, everyone accepted Chie's logic.

He put three handfuls of deer jerky into his pouch.
He put a handful of cartridges beside the dried meat.
Then he added a small leather sack that held his war
medicine.

Chie had a lump of turquoise carved by a Zuni into
the shape of a bear. That was his hunting charm. Next
there was a small splinter from an oak that had been

struck by lightning. Lastly, the shriveled finger of a gold prospector whom he had helped torture to death east of Fort Bowie two years before.

He picked up the Springfield and began to run at a fast trot.

Slocum emerged from the canyon just at sunrise. To the south, bare brown ridges stretched as far as he could see. The breeze had died when the sun rose, as if on cue. The sun began to glare from the hot sand wherever it flowed around the isolated boulders. The only vegetation was the low scrub of creosote bush, which shimmered away endlessly as far as they could see.

Occasionally, between ridges, they came to bare washes which were sometimes a mile across. Covered with gravel, and with the water table far below, nothing grew there. On this series of ridge after ridge there was nothing alive. Slocum looked at it with pleasure. If he could find such land all the way to the border he might very well escape all Apache attacks.

The wind was right. The deer came out of the oaks, lifted its head, smelled for whatever enemies might be sending scent to it: cougar, bear, human. Not smelling anything, he lowered his head and began drinking from the pine-fringed pond.

Chie pulled the trigger. The blast bruised his shoulder, but he had remembered to squeeze the trigger. He had aimed badly. He did not know anything about elevating or lowering sights. Still, his slug smashed the deer's shoulder blade. He could not run, and he collapsed. When Chie stood over him he flailed with his hooves at the human, but Chie waited patiently until the deer died from loss of blood.

Chie was not after venison. He wanted the deer's intestine. This he took, after first squeezing out all its half-digested contents. Satisfied, he coiled it and placed it in his pouch. He would have use for it, for he had seen the tracks of the two Belighanna going into the desert.

A small, narrow creek wandered across the table-land, and then flowed downhill toward the desert. There it disappeared into the loose gravel. But Chie knew that a mile from its last appearance it made a small pool that was four feet deep.

At the pool he took out the coil and tied one end in a hard knot. He held open the other end and slowly let the entire length fill with water. When that had been accomplished, he coiled its long length about his lean, hard brown torso several times.

Now he had a very big canteen on which he could survive for six days of the most strenuous running under the furnace of the desert sun.

Danny said, "No one's seen hide nor hair of them two."

"Where'd you ask?" Gill said.

"Hung 'round Hunter's kitchen, sweet-talkin' the cook. Looked in the stable. Their horses ain't back. Ol' guv'nor can't figger out what happened to Hoffman 'n' McDermott, that little prick bastard. Sometimes he wants t' send deppities out, other times he figgers word'll come in from one of the sheriffs 'round the Territory. He sent telegrams 'n' letters to all of 'em. No one ain't seen the missus."

"No one said that feller that took Molly Hunter is stupid."

"She says the guv'nor wants 'er back real bad."

"Me too," Gill said.

Danny felt a cold wave slide up his spine when he saw Gill's smile. He said, "Poole ain't back yet? Ain't seen 'im 'round."

Gill did not respond.

"Jim neither, hey?"

"No!" Gill snapped.

"So," Danny said quietly, "none of them four is back."

The thought had not yet occurred to Gill. The impact of Danny's questions suddenly hit him.

Had the four men joined forces? That was what Gill would do if he were in their shoes; it seemed perfectly natural to combine forces and thus avoid being shot by the other pair.

Had they caught up with Slocum and grabbed the letters? Maybe. Had they killed Molly Hunter in order to eliminate her, if she had seen the two forces merge? Gill immediately believed that was what had happened. And the reason, he said to himself, why he hadn't heard from them—and why Hunter hadn't heard—was that they were planning how to use the letters to blackmail both him and Hunter.

The more he thought about it, the more he felt his theory was not a theory but the truth.

There was only one way to handle it. Gill told Danny to saddle his horse and stuff plenty of food in the saddlebags. While he went upstairs to change he told Danny to roust out two new men he had just put on as replacements on a temporary basis until Poole and Blunt returned. They were hired killers from Montana who had spent a couple of months killing small ranchers who had been branding the maverick stock of the great northern ranches. Several indictments had been handed down and they had ridden away. They needed a job badly and would do just about anything for steady work, now that winter was coming.

Gill had no doubt whatsoever that he would spoil Poole's little scheme. He'd kill that son of a bitch Slocum as well—slowly, the Apache way—and that would solve the goddamn letter problem. Molly would have to go too, if the others hadn't yet done it. None of this would have happened if she hadn't written those letters to start with. It was her fault.

When he had buckled on his gunbelt the two men showed up. He looked at their hard faces. "Got a little job for you," Gill said. "Might involve a little . . . you know." He waggled his hand.

"No hay problema," one of them said, with a yawn.

Gill smiled.

Governor Hunter said, "And send out those telegrams once more. This time offer a reward of ten thousand dollars."

"What!"

"Ten thousand, god damn it!"

"Yes, sir."

"Make sure the governors of Chihuahua and Sonora get the telegrams. Mark them for personal attention. Those greasers sure are greedy for dollars."

"Yes, sir."

"And, Raymond—"

"Yes, sir?"

"On the way to the telegraph office I want to see your coattails out so straight I can serve a six-course dinner on 'em. Understand?"

"Yes, sir."

As they moved deeper inside the range they moved to higher elevations. It was high desert country, with cactus the dominant plant. There came a perfect network of precipices. Small streams issued from the rock walls, flowed together, and formed a river that flowed through the dry, dead mountains. Sometimes sandstone cliffs surged upward for a thousand feet, although the average, Slocum judged, was two to three hundred. From the top of the taller cliffs the river looked like a silver snake. It kept twisting from side to side, as if trying to climb the narrow walls that hemmed it in.

At every bend it took, a little horseshoe-shaped flat of level ground was formed opposite to where it splashed against the cliffs. One day they forded the river seventeen times.

Once, while letting the horses drink, Slocum looked up. A tiny figure was looking down at them. As Slocum watched it disappeared. Molly did not notice it.

They were being shadowed. The constant fording of the river slowed them down enormously. Apaches on foot on the rim could move in a straight line and easily keep pace with them, even if Slocum and Molly constantly changed to fresh horses. And sooner or later the attack would come, in a manner they would not expect. He would have to move against the Apache on the rim; he and Molly were sitting ducks.

•   •   •

Chie saw that the precipice ahead dropped down to the hundred-foot level. He trotted ahead. He removed the deer intestine; it still remained one third full of water. He peered over the edge. The Belighanna were almost there. Chie lay flat, placed a cartridge in the chamber, and shoved the bolt home.

Squeeze, they had said, *squeeze*.

He lined up Slocum in his sights. Unwittingly, he had done the right thing for a man who had no idea how to use the weapon properly. He did not have to allow for the bullet's drop in its flight.

He squeezed.

The *boom* of the Springfield filled the narrow canyon with its blast. The bullet buried itself in the back of Slocum's cantle. The force of the impact knocked his hips forward three inches. The horses plunged and bucked.

By the time Chie could reload, Slocum had pulled the horses under an overhang on the same side of the canyon, under the cliff Chie had fired from.

"Jesus, that was *close*," Slocum said.

He sat down and took off his boots. She looked at him as if he were crazy. His woolen stockings would protect his feet. He made sure the carbine was loaded. She paled when she realized what he intended to do.

"What—" she began. It was hard for her to go on. "What if—"

"Listen to me, Molly. He'll be doing that all day. He almost busted my spine. He's gonna hit me. Or you. Springfields make an awful big hole. And you're too pretty to be smashed up. So I'm going up there and make a hole in him."

"I—"

"You'll have four horses to change to, Molly. Most people only have one. You'll be in fine shape. There's gold in the saddlebags, so you'll get a good start down in Mexico. Go to Chihuahua. If I were you I'd open up a good cathouse. Before you do anything, go see the governor of the state, Antonio Molinos. Say you're a good friend of mine. He owes me a favor. Tell him the whole story from the beginning, when you met Joe Gill. *All*. He will see that nothing happens to you. He will protect your place."

"What place?"

"Why, Molly, your cathouse."

"My *what?*"

"You'd be good at it, Molly. The idea that the wife of a gringo governor is running a *casa* in Mexico—listen, Molly, every Mexican with money to spend is gonna love the idea of screwing in Molly Hunter's whorehouse."

In spite of her fear, she began to smile.

He made sure the carbine was loaded.

"You're going to climb that cliff?" she asked.

"Molly, you just remember what I said, and give me a kiss for good luck."

She flung her arms around him and thrust her tongue deep in his mouth. Slocum suddenly had a violent erection, much to his surprise. Under the tension of the trip he had not thought about sex at all.

"I'll be back, Molly," he told her.

"You better."

Slocum smiled. He stepped out from under the overhang and looked up. As he had figured, there was a black-haired man up there looking down. Slocum lifted his carbine and fired three shots. Pieces of sandstone chipped off the very edge of the rim. That would keep the bastard's head down for a few minutes.

Slocum ran along the cliff until he came to an area where it was not a true vertical. There were outcrops and slits and an occasional bush growing out of the rock. He had made a sling for the carbine out of a length of riata. He slung it across his back and began climbing with such expertise and speed that Molly was reminded of mountain sheep she had seen moving on seemingly impossible surfaces.

She watched with fascination as he climbed. His fingers and toes found handholds and toeholds that were invisible from the canyon floor; it seemed to Molly that he was going up like a deadly spider.

He had told her to fire three more shots at the rim when he was almost at the top. She did this now.

Half a minute later he waved at her and slid over the rim, out of sight. She bit her forefinger to keep from crying in fear.

Slocum slid over the edge and froze to immobility.

The flat top of the cliff was littered with boulders. He had come out between two of them. He inched forward. Completely shielded by one of them, he risked a look to his right.

He saw a strange Apache a hundred and fifty feet away. Chie was flat on his back, with his arms folded. The Springfield, which Slocum recognized as having belonged to Thankful Smith, lay by his side. Chie was smiling. There was no way for Slocum to understand the smile, but if Chie could have spoken to Slocum he would have said, "I almost got you last time. My aim is getting better. Next time I will hit you right on the top of your skull. The small Belighanna will be easy to take prisoner, not like you. I will tie him to his horse and bring him back to the Black Range. With luck, he will last a day under my knife. Then I will have two carbines as well as Colts.

"Sooner or later he will have to go to sleep. Then I will have him. He is heading for Mexico, but the horses need water. As soon as he leaves the river, I will run far ahead of him and wait for him at Arroyo Seco. When he waters the horses I will jump on him from the big stone above the pool. It will be easy.

"But now I will wait till they look away. It is better that I move along the rim fifty feet or so before I look over."

Chie got to his feet, crouched, picked up his Springfield, turned, and saw Slocum standing ten feet from him. Slocum's carbine was pointing at his heart. The first thing that registered with Chie was that the Belighanna was not wearing boots. Blood had soaked through his torn stockings. Chie thought: *This Belighanna came up the cliff; he is smarter than I am.*

Although he knew it was hopeless, he swung his Springfield around. Slocum fired one shot. It smashed Chie's trigger finger, went through his palm, and screeched away across the cliff top. The shock made him drop the Springfield. Chie dropped to his knees, then sat cross-legged. He held his bleeding hand in his left palm while he began the low, monotonous chant Slocum recognized as his death song.

He was waiting for the shot through the heart.

Slocum had seen enough dead men lately. He hesitated. He saw the long deer intestine. He knew what it was for. He took out his knife and slashed it through several times. It would be completely useless for its purpose, which he knew was for a canteen. Chie would be unable to follow them across the desert stretch.

Chie watched this with calm acceptance while he chanted.

Slocum reached into Chie's pouch and removed the eight Springfield cartridges that remained. He shoved them into his pockets.

The rifle was undamaged.

Slocum said, "I am going down the cliff. I will leave these cartridges at our camp."

Chie stopped his chant abruptly. So the strange Belighanna was not going to kill him.

"You owe me one life," Slocum said. "If I come back again to the Black Range, remember that."

Chie looked at him, expressionless. The pain suddenly struck him and he bent over in agony. Then he straightened, ashamed that he had shown weakness to this amazing man.

The man was waiting for an answer. Chie nodded. He had given his word; Slocum knew he could rely on that. He had provided himself with insurance when he returned for the nuggets some day.

Slocum turned and walked away. Now that the man was out of hearing, Chie allowed himself a moan of agony. But at least the Belighanna had left him his Springfield and the eight cartridges.

12

Governor Antonio Quesada Molinos sat in his office and watched with a big grin as Slocum and Molly walked in.

He leaped to his feet, hugged Slocum, kissed him on both cheeks, and yelled, *"Como le va, cabrón!"*

"O.K.," Slocum said, smiling. Molinos hugged him again.

Molly watched with amusement. She was dressed in a black skirt and white blouse and a gold chain necklace.

"And who is this charming lady?"

"This is Molly Hunter," Slocum said without preamble, "the wife of Governor Hunter of New Mexico. She wants to open a whorehouse here in Chihuahua."

"Jesus Christ and all the saints!" Molinos said,

"You never fail to amaze me, you crazy son of a bitch!"

Molly relaxed; only very good friends were permitted to call each other that.

"I forget my manners!" the governor said. "Catalina!"

The Indian maid padded in barefoot. "Catalina, bring the champagne. Be sure it is cold!"

The maid giggled and withdrew.

"Champagne?" Slocum asked.

"Much different from old days, eh? In the old days we drank stale *pulque.*" He sighed. "I miss them, don't you?"

Slocum nodded.

The governor turned to Molly. *"Señora,"* he said, "in the old days, what was I? A poor *bandido.* There was a bad governor here in Chihuahua. I gathered men to me, but what could I do about the guns the governor had? Very little. My men had spades and sticks. So I held some *hacendado* for ransom, with the money I went to Texas for guns. Everyone I talked to I somehow did not trust. I had some fear; yes, I, Antonio Quesada Molinos, admit it.

"Then I met this *cabrón.* He said very little. And the next thing I knew, I had everything I needed— guns, ammunition. All in fine condition, even better than he said they would be. I needed three thousand dollars more, and he said he would trust me. This I never forgot. So we had a little revolution in Chihuahua, and my price to Mexico City to stop it was to make me the new governor. And it was done. So that is why I now drink champagne. You like it?" he asked anxiously.

"Superb," she said. "Even New Orleans has none better."

He bowed with pleasure, then turned to Slocum. "Of course, your lady can open a whorehouse. I shall be honored. I shall make sure that she is not bothered by *anyone*. I will waive the usual opening fee. Consider it done."

Slocum said, "*Gracias,* Tonio."

The governor shrugged. Then he leaned across his desk and picked up a telegram. He grinned and handed it to Slocum.

"That's an easy ten thousand," Slocum said.

The Governor laughed. "*Amigo mio,* we have done such things together! Only worms care for money."

Slocum passed the telegram to Molly. "He really wants me back," she said. "Or is it the letters?"

"You make the decision on that," Slocum said as he sipped the champagne.

"It's the goddamn letters," she said.

The governor held up another telegram. "Listen to this, Slocum," he said. "The *Federales* patrolling the south side of the border near Ojinaga have caught two Americans who say they are looking for the man who kidnapped the wife of Governor Hunter. They do not like their looks; they look like bad men. They would like to shoot them as a matter of principle. They say they work for a man named Gill in Santa Fe. They say they are doing this for this Gill because Gill wants to be a good citizen and help his friend the governor. What is your opinion?"

"Shoot them while attempting to escape," Slocum said coldly.

The governor looked at him fondly. "I knew you

would say that, *amigo,* so I will order it done. You
will remain here as my guest until we find a fine house
for the *señora.* And I·will tell all my rich friends about
this interesting new house run by the wife of a governor! They will love it. I will instruct every *alcalde*
in the state of Chihuahua to locate and recommend
only the cleanest and prettiest girls for you, *señora!"*

"*Muchas gracias.*"

"You must practice your Spanish, *señora.* I am told
you came into Chihuahua with much gold, Slocum."

"Ah, rumors, rumors."

The governor grinned. They knew each other well.

"If you should need help getting more of it, let me
know. I know many men who owe me and you large
favors."

"Should the need come, I will be grateful, Tonio."

"And now, we shall go out to dine in a fine French
restaurant. Yes, *señora,* there is one here, with a French
chef as good as any in New Orleans. I have told him
that if the cooking falls off, I will shoot him."

Molly laughed with pleasure. She did not know
that Molinos was speaking accurately.

The food was superb.

That afternoon, a huge rainstorm hit the Sangre de
Cristo range, to the east of Santa Fe. The Santa Fe
River, which flowed out of the range, was the river
beside which Slocum had hidden the letters under a
boulder.

No one expected such a storm at this time of the
year, not even the old residents. The river rose eight
feet above its usual height. There was much damage
in downtown Santa Fe. The water flowed down the

streets and some of it entered Joe Gill's saloon and filled his basement.

He did much cursing at Danny as he supervised the mopping and bailing out. But he did not know, nor did the governor in his Palace, that the huge, powerful current had rolled over the boulder on top of the letters. The water seized the package, rolled it over and over, and finally tore it open on a sharp branch from a willow tree that had collapsed into the raging torrent. The letters poured out. Soaked, they became soft; the current sent them boiling up and down, tearing them gradually into tiny fragments. By the time the Santa Fe River reached the massive, calm brown flow of the Rio Grande as it moved calmly to the Gulf of Mexico, no one could ever know that the letters had ever existed.

JAKE LOGAN

___ 07139-1	**SOUTH OF THE BORDER**	$2.50
___ 07567-2	**SLOCUM'S PRIDE**	$2.50
___ 07382-3	**SLOCUM AND THE GUN-RUNNERS**	$2.50
___ 07494-3	**SLOCUM'S WINNING HAND**	$2.50
___ 08382-9	**SLOCUM IN DEADWOOD**	$2.50
___ 07654-7	**SLOCUM'S STAMPEDE**	$2.50
___ 07973-2	**SLOCUM AND THE AVENGING GUN**	$2.50
___ 08087-0	**THE SUNSHINE BASIN WAR**	$2.50
___ 08279-2	**VIGILANTE JUSTICE**	$2.50
___ 08189-3	**JAILBREAK MOON**	$2.50
___ 08392-6	**SIX GUN BRIDE**	$2.50
___ 08076-5	**MESCALERO DAWN**	$2.50
___ 08539-6	**DENVER GOLD**	$2.50
___ 08644-X	**SLOCUM AND THE BOZEMAN TRAIL**	$2.50
___ 08742-5	**SLOCUM AND THE HORSE THIEVES**	$2.50
___ 08773-5	**SLOCUM AND THE NOOSE OF HELL**	$2.50
___ 08791-3	**CHEYENNE BLOODBATH**	$2.50
___ 09088-4	**THE BLACKMAIL EXPRESS**	$2.50
___ 09111-2	**SLOCUM AND THE SILVER RANCH FIGHT**	$2.50
___ 09299-2	**SLOCUM AND THE LONG WAGON TRAIN**	$2.50

162b

J.D. HARDIN

"THE MOST EXCITING WESTERN WRITER SINCE LOUIS L'AMOUR"
—JAKE LOGAN